The Quest

Book ❶_Adela

The QueSt Book❶_ Adela

초판 1쇄 인쇄   2014년 08월 12일
초판 1쇄 발행   2014년 08월 18일

지은이   최 민 경
펴낸이   손 형 국
펴낸곳   (주)북랩
편집인   선일영   편집   이소현, 이윤채, 김아름, 이탄석
디자인   이현수, 신혜림, 김루리   제작   박기성, 황동현, 구성우
마케팅   김회란, 이희정
출판등록   2004. 12. 1(제2012-000051호)
주소   서울시 금천구 가산디지털 1로 168, 우림라이온스밸리 B동 B113, 114호
홈페이지   www.book.co.kr
전화번호   (02)2026-5777   팩스   (02)2026-5747

ISBN   979-11-5585-310-8 04810 (종이책)   979-11-5585-311-5 04810 (set)
                979-11-5585-322-1 05810 (전자책)

이 도서의 국립중앙도서관 출판시도서목록(CIP)은 서지정보유통지원시스템 홈페이지(http://seoji.nl.go.kr)와
국가자료공동목록시스템(http://www.nl.go.kr/kolisnet)에서 이용하실 수 있습니다.
(CIP제어번호: CIP 2014023665)

The Quest

Book ❶_ Adela

최민경 지음

북랩 book Lab

추천사

The Quest는 신화적인 틀을 차용하면서 학교라는 현실 공간에서 이루어지는 청소년들의 우정과 질투, 사랑, 화해, 그리고 때로는 어른스러운 사회적 주제들까지 다루는 흥미로운 성장소설입니다. 특히, 등장인물들의 심리묘사나 대화는 어른 작가가 흉내 내기 어려울 만큼 그들 만의 세계와 생각을 그들의 관점에서 생동감 있게 잘 그려내고 있는 점이 인상적입니다. 그러나 그 무엇보다도 주인공 찰스와 아델라의 사랑을 영어라는 표현수단을 통해 긴장감을 잃지 않으며 이렇게 멋지게 담아내는 고등학생 저자의 문학적 상상력과 표현력이 매우 유쾌합니다.

숙명여대 영문학부 **이형진 교수**

추천사

The Quest depicts a story that is sentimental, full of infinite imagination and a tasteful sense of expression which was generated from a high school girl's delicate emotion. The writer's brilliant intelligence is presented through her novel which considerates reflection of the society and mankind. Once you concentrate on Adela's thrilled challenge to become the Queen, you will find yourself enamored with the novel and supporting Adela's adventure.

이화의대 산부인과학교실 **주웅 교수**

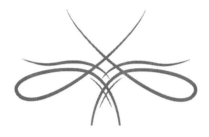

To my loving family
who always stood behind me
with patience, trust and love
And to myself
who struggled for 5 years,
building my dream into reality

Contents

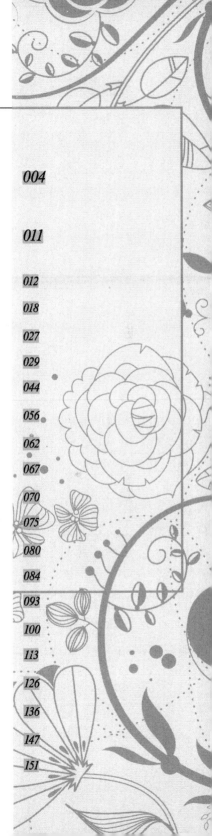

PART 1

Adela

'One's will to live'

Extraordinary, to start with

Adela, this is my name. It actually means 'one's will to live' and has a lot of stories in it.

Where should I start first? It was snowing in Anastelon at the first time of the year when I was born. The windows got almost frozen by the water that the cleaner Jackie spread on the windows using his old tin bucket to clean the windows that were almost dustless, but cold. The sun was hiding behind the puffy clouds and was hardly showing its light.

"When I held you with my both arms for the first time," My father said, sipping the brandy from his favorite silvery cup. Then, he took a moment and said, "When I held you softly as I can as I thought of what to name you, you stretched your tiny hand out and touched the frozen glass and your hand twitched with cold. I remember every exact movement that you did on that day. I knew that you are extraordinary, Adel."

This was what he firstly said to me after I read about our secret clan and our enemies. He said that when I asked, "How was I when I was born, father?"

I still remember the time I touched the silvery and soft cover of the book about our secret clan and our enemies. I got that book for my birthday when I became 5 years old.

I learned a lot from it. I felt so amazed finding out that I was very different from others. I was not human.

I was an Aian clan's princess, who would be the queen next year as I turn 18, which means that I would become an adult and marry a dumb old prince which is the part that I mostly hate.

My father told me other things that made me feel so proud and amused of myself.

"You are an Aian, so you can transform into different kinds of animals when it's time." My father told me this when our royal family was eating dinner. And I, little Adela was so surprised at this that she almost swallowed the whole chunk of the meat from the table and choked so loudly that it echoed through the hall. Haha, yes, this got me into serious trouble that was called 'Learning how to be well-mannered from a guy who I do not know what he is called'. He became my teacher after what had happened to me. My tidiest queen mother frowned at me choking and spitting out the chunk of meat. My mother and father did not stand up nor did anything because they did not want to be impatient and rude. They just sat down and finished their dinner a little quicker than usual. Then, they ordered a servant to call an expert of manners.

Wow, I know. I can transform into animals...All right. That sounds amazing.

But the fact is, I have never done the transforming yet in my entire 18 years of living.

And I read it from the book about some more amazing things which made me gasp as I read it down interestedly with my eyes wide open.

Those four inky words, written on the ancient paper, said,

"Aians have two lives."

I almost used one of my lives. My mother told me that I almost lost my first life when I was just 6 years old. I was trying to fly off the top of Mekhaim Tower.

That time, one of my close maids Brianna was holding a wooden orange basket full of laundries and was walking to the laundry room in the corner of our kingdom, right next to the tower. She was humming her favorite song and was walking across the land. Then, she accidently looked up and saw what was happening. She dropped her basket and screamed.

"Oh no, princess no!" She tried to run up the tower, but it was impossible to climb up the tower that has two thousand and thirty six stairs to reach the top and save me, who was about to jump off.

"Fly high to the sky, I've decided, don't ask why!"

This makes no sense, but I was so young back then, and I thought I could transform into a bird and I knew, I mean I thought I knew that it was time.

I could somehow feel that it was time with my both arms, stretched out on each side and the freezing wind, brushing my hair towards its track. I looked down and felt the gentle heart of our village Anastelon that was right below me, which made me brave without fearing that it was too high for me to stand on.

But, I had no fear. Actually, I could not fear anything.

"I can do this." I told myself over and over and looked down again.

Now there were my mother and father, staring up at me with their each both eyes, feeling worried and angry at the same time. Right away, my father told my mother to stay there and started to climb up the stairs with other soldiers and maids.

"Adel!" My mother sobbed and kept shouting as loud as she could, but this time, she forgot about the rule number fifty six, which was called, "Do not shout or yell at someone even if they did something to distract you."

My heart felt like it was torn apart as I saw my mother cry for the first time. I hesitated for a moment. My decision started to weaken and I could hear the footsteps of my father and other people behind me. I did not know what to do.

My mother was sobbing, my father was climbing up the stairs as fast as he could and I felt like they were squeezing me. The wind started to blow strongly, the sun seemed to be hidden behind the clouds and I could find some grey pigeons flapping their wide wings and soaring across the sky. So, I smiled and made the decision.

I jumped off the tower, at last.

That was when my father reached the top of the tower with those people, all out of breath. My father reached for my leg but failed to catch it. I closed my eyes and widen my shoulders and stretched out my arms. I flapped my arms as fast as I could, but I felt my body sucking into the ground, then, I felt myself, sinking into something, leaving my heart floating in the air and then there was a large bang below me and everything was too silent for me to hear my pigeons making flapping sounds with their wings.

And nothing was visible.

I was floating in the air with something below me as I suddenly realized that every part of my body was numb and cranky. I felt like my spirit was out of my body and my body was a chunk of corpse. My eyelids were too heavy for me to open, as if there were huge boulders covering them. I started to lose my capacity as I pushed and shoved my body using all my power I had. However, nothing there was I could hear or touch.

"Oh, please Adel." This was the first words that I heard as I tried to move my legs as far as they could go. My heart started to bounce like I was about to win a medal. Then, I peeked through my blurry eyelids that were half opened.

"Oh please, do not worry, your highness," I could hear another voice coming from my left side of where I was. I used all my left power to move my arm to show the movements to prove that I was not dead, but all it did was to twitch a little.

"Miss Adela just had broken her left arm, two ribs and her right ankle. That is all and she did not get any more damage than that. Also, she fell into the laundry basket, and thanks to that, she's still alive and breathing,"

I heard my mother sob harder than before I saw her at the tower. I felt heartbroken and tried to reach her face to wipe her tears off her pale face. But, my arms were too stubborn to move.

"Don't worry, your highness, if she was human like me, she would have been too weak to live in this accident. It was such a miracle not losing one of her lives."

I listened to every sound and by the time the silence reached the room, I made a groan as loudly as I could. And then, I opened my eyes slowly and stared at my mother's startled face and smiled gently. Then I opened my mouth to speak.

"Mother, I… am okay." I murmured and then stared at my father, who was standing right next to my mother, rubbing my mother's shoulder with his hand. My mother's eyes went wide and her mouth got round. She hugged me as tightly as she could like she was not letting me go for ever. My father quickly came to us and smoothed my hair. Everyone let out a joyful squeal and everything was all right after that..... Until I became eighteen.

Normal School Life

I peeked through my eyelids as Brianna rang the small bell that she always has in her pocket of her white apron. She swung it around and closed the door as she came in.

"Wake up, my dear lazy princess!" She shouted and reached for the curtains to side them to let the fresh sunlight come in. As usual, I quickly buried my face in my squishy pillow and closed my eyes tightly as I could. However, Brianna rang the bell as strongly and loudly as she could, which made me burst out of my bed hastily.

"Adela," I mumbled as I rubbed my eyes to see clearer. "You can call me Adela, Brie, just like I call you with your name. I know I am a princess, but it is too…heavy and…um, you know, 'princessy'."

I made a word up and sit back down on the bed and stretched. Brianna made a face and stared at me like I do not have a clue what I was saying.

"Ma'am," She said to me with her tone, mixed with anger. "It is true that I am your closest maid but I think you, miss, are misunderstanding me as a friend."

I sighed in a prankish way and grinned at Brianna to make her feel happier. At last, Brianna's eyebrow twitched and slowly her mouth stretched up. My tummy began to roar and echoed in the fluffy blanket.

"Oh, Brianna, what is for breakfast?" I asked. Brianna's face lit up and hurried to the door and looked back at me as she grabbed the door knob.

"What would you like to have for breakfast miss?" She asked, "Scrambled egg, bacon and toast or crusty chunk of bread with cheese and butter?"

"Cheese and bread please and don't forget the butter." I said and gazed at Brianna hurrying down the kitchen. I waited and waited blank-mindedly.

5 minutes later, Brianna came carefully with a chunk of bread and a lot of cheese and butter and a glass of fresh milk. My mouth began to water. As she gently put down the plate on my blanket-covered knees, I started to squish them into my mouth.

"Whoa whoa, miss Adela. Mind your manners." Brianna said, laughing softly.

I chewed the bread and the yellow cheese slowly without spitting them out. Then, I quickly headed to the bathroom.

"Is Michael out there waiting?" I asked as I squeezed the tube to brush my teeth.

Brianna thought for a moment.

"Um, actually, Mr. Henderson is out there waiting for you miss and he said that he will walk with you to the school for today." Brianna yelled to me and folded the blanket. I choked.

"Oh my goodness! Is he?" I squealed of delight and quickly brushed my teeth and ran to my dressing room and put my clothes on real quickly and grabbed my bag.

"Bye mother, bye father. I am going to school now." I said as I opened the gate.

Lowell was standing there with his cool blue colored clothes. His dark blonde hair brushing aside as the wind swished around him.

Lowell looked up at me and grinned.

"Hey," He let out a gentle laugh that I loved to hear. "Come on down."

I softly smiled back at him and ran down the stairs. Then, we headed to the street and started talking to each other.

"So, how was your vacation?" He asked, staring at me.

"Boring as usual." I said with my eyes, half-closed.

Lowell's eyebrow moved up like he was confused.

"Adela, you are one of the royal family, your life would be way better than a normal guy's like mine."

I sighed and opened my mouth. "Are we just going to walk to school or take a bus?"

Lowell chuckled unnoticeably. "Do you even know that we are late?"

I gasped and looked at my watch and bit my lip. "Great." I muttered at last.

We walked faster and arrived at school 15 minutes later. The first period bell rang and as I got to my locker. I took out my Math notebook and my pencil case and went down there to meet my other friend Cathy.

"Hey," She called me and waved her arm for me to see her.

My eyes caught her unusual dress in red and black stripes and waved to her back. Her silky ginger funky hair flew as she ran to me in her biggest smile.

"Hey, miss Adela princess! Long time no see!" She yelled.

"Yeah, we had not seen each other since we became 17. We were in different classes."

Her chin slightly went up and we walked down the hall.

She stared down at my math notebook and squealed.

"Oh my god, we have the same subject in next period!" She said. "We are going to be in the same class together."

I smiled and stared at her green eyes and nodded.

"Oh, and I have seen you walking with Lowell, Adela," She whispered to me, which made my face to go scarlet.

"We just met," I lied really quickly. "We are just friends, I swear, no more than that. I just think him as my best friend."

"Then, why would your face go red huh? I know, he is gorgeous isn't he? I am definitely in love with him." She stared into my eyes and squinted. I sighed and grinned at her.

We finally stopped in front of class 12 and sat down in the front aisle next to each other. Then, I heard the door shut and Ms. Kimberly came in with the loud noises of her high stiletto shoes that shined as she walked. Her brown eyes glanced at everyone and her red skirt that came down by her knees fluttered.

"Hello everyone," She said in a delightful voice. "I am so happy to meet you guys all and I am going to be teaching you math, which is going to be the most important subject of all this semester."

She let out an unconvincing cough and added, "I am human, as you all would know and I am very different from some of you."

I knew that math would be very boring. I sighed and daydreamed as Ms. Kimberly kept saying about what she likes and what she is going to teach us and some more facts about herself. She kept talking and talking and all of the students started to get bored except Cathy. Her eyes stared straight into Ms. Kimberly's eyes and she looked like she was staring at something that is very rare and complex.

"When I was a little kid, I was the greatest in math, so I got a lot of attention from teachers." She said and tapped her book with her ball point pen and caught a glimpse on me. Her friendly face suddenly, hardened and she dropped her pen. Everything went silent. I gulped and tried to make my head low as possible. She stared at me for a long time and made an unnoticeable huge smile on her pale face; the smile that looked like a wolf had caught a juicy fat deer without even touching it. Suddenly, the bell rang and Ms. Kimberly blinked in surprise.

"Oh, the bell!" Her face contorted into her kind smile again and she stood up. "We did nothing today except listening to me babbling on myself, haven't we? I am very sorry if the stories were boring, but listening to someone very patiently is a development that we made. Good job everyone."

She swished her hand around to sign to us to go, but Ms. Kimberly's eyes were only on me and I felt like something was poking me with disgrace. I shivered and ran out of the room quickly.

Cathy ran out after me. "Whoa, she was a chunk of bore, wasn't she? My favorite subject was math, but it will not be until this semester ends!"

I glanced at her and let out a sigh.

This pretty much predicted my day in school. History was boring, fitness was delayed and French was not interesting or easy. Time kept flying and flying until I met Cathy and Lowell in the hall in front of room 9. Lowell looked as if he just chewed on the yuckiest food. He swung his hand which was holding his yellow lunch bag around to wake me up from daydreaming into the space.

"Adela," He said in his tired voice. "Come on, it's lunch time."

I looked up at him and smiled gently. Cathy held my hand and pulled me toward the cafeteria.

We sat down somewhere in the corner and I went down to the counter to get my lunch with Cathy. Cathy ran next to me with her plate and leaned over me.

"Oh my, I think he is a little interested in me," She said blushing like a strawberry. "He stared at me for about 10 seconds. I am totally sure. Oh my god, what am I going to do?" Cathy jumped up and down, looking at Lowell, who was staring into space, chewing on his handful sandwich.

I turned around and looked at him and glanced at my plate. Then, I laughed gently. "Oh, come on Cathy. There would be no change for you and him when he looks at you or something. He is your friend. He thinks of you as you think of me."

"He is not just an ordinary friend, Adela," She said as she glanced at him again. "He is my friend who I have a crush on. I feel like, I cannot even live without him."

"Can you girls quickly walk past for some students behind you?" Mrs. Grains yelled with her scratchy voice and spinned around to get some more spoons. We looked up and hurried down our trail and grabbed the wrapped sandwich from the bowl and moved on to the other bowl to take a little carton of milk. Then, Cathy and I walked back to our table and sat down in front of Lowell.

Lowell's silky hair swished over his head as he looked up.

"Hey," He said smiling. "Why did it take so long? I mean, it took about 5 minutes for you guys to grab a sandwich and a carton of milk for each of you and to come back."

Cathy blushed again and we began to eat.

I bit into my sandwich and I could taste the juicy tuna and the mayonnaise that were mixed together nicely. As I swallowed and bit into it once more, my saliva started to gain more. But I suddenly remembered the sharp glimpse from Ms. Kimberly. I frowned as I thought about her.

"What's wrong Adela? You look a little pissed off." Lowell scowled.

I stared at them and leaned over to them across the table. Then I faced Cathy.

"Cathy," I said with my serious eyes. "Have you spotted Ms. Kimberly gazing at me during class?"

Cathy rolled her eyes and clicked her fingers silently.

"I was wondering about that in class because she was staring at something for a long time. I was guessing if she was looking at you when I followed her eyes, but I did not really care about it."

"Ms. Kimberly?" Lowell said, taking another bite of his red apple. "I think I saw her in the school office this morning when I went there to enroll after-school programs. Isn't she the one with blondish brown hair with all those make-ups? She seems new to this school."

"You mean those red glowing lipstick and pink visible blushers?" Cathy snorted and grinned. "Yeah, totally. She needs to get a proper make-up. Even I would say that Lindsay's make-up is much better than hers."

Lindsay? You are saying that? No way is Cathy saying that.

Lindsay is the most popular girl in our school, and I don't want to admit the fact that she wears all those fancy new clothes from famous brands. Well, my friends thought that I could possibly get whatever I want since I was the 'princess', and I thought that was true too, until the king, my father told me not to spend too much money on shopping. It is so unfair. Why am I not like a princess in a fairytale?

"What? Are you talking that fancy Lindsay Allen wears better make-up?" I laughed hard and stared at Cathy. "No way no way no way you are saying that!"

"Excuse me?" Suddenly, a squeaky voice came behind me. All of us three looked up. There was Lindsay, standing in her crazy hot pink stiletto heels and wearing dark velvet sweater and a purple miniskirt. Her group of friends stood behind her staring down at the three.

"Excuse me losers, and I almost forgot, my precious little Princess

Monette. And what did you just say, my dear princess?"

I swallowed, and I told myself; Stay cool Adela, you can do it. Just tell her to shut up and go away. I can do it.

I opened my mouth. "Well, I just said to my friends that your make-up is the worst of our school."

Everyone's mouth made a shape like an 'o' and the whole cafeteria turned quiet. All of the sudden, there was no noise and kids did not even dare to take a breath. All we could hear was the clinging sound of the pot in the kitchen.

I swallowed again and glared at Lindsay. Lindsay sharply glared at me back and snorted at me.

"Huh, I have never known Miss Princess can say all those things about me. How dare you insult me behind my back with your friends?"

I clenched my jaws tightly and the anger flew.

"Yes, of course I can say all those insults because you deserve them."

"Oh, yeah Adela?" she said with her scowling face. "But right now, I am getting insults from only three of you, but forever after, you and your two stupid friends, of course, will get teased, bullied by everyone and get kicked out of the school. I promise that would happen soon, very soon."

Lindsay swung back and led her group out of the cafeteria. Then, the silence broke right after Lindsay pushed the last foot out of the cafeteria.

I sighed and turned back to my friends. Cathy and Lowell did not say anything, looking down at their lunches.

Headaches

I came back from school and went upstairs to my room. When I opened the door of my room, I threw my bag messily and threw myself to the comfy bed.

That time, Brianna came out of the bathroom with dusty rugs and saw me lying on my bed. She was surprised to see me without any noise, so she ran to me leaving all the dirty rugs on the floor.

"Miss Princess! Are you all right? Do you have a cold or do you feel sick or anything?"

"No Brianna, I am fine, just that, I don't have good feelings about school, that's all."

Brianna covered her mouth and shook her hands in a shock.

"Oh, should I cancel math tutoring, ballet dancing and basketball today? If your highness feels tired, there is no problem canceling any of them. What should I do?"

"No no Brie, stay calm. I am all right okay? My body can do all those works for today, except my mind does not want to."

Brianna laughed softly and picked up the rugs scattered around the floor.

"Okay, but please take a rest before the tutor comes and if you have any problems, ring the bell." Brianna disappeared out of her room and walked down the stairs.

I sighed and buried my face to my feather pillow. Such a weird day today, I thought. Who is this mysterious Ms. Kimberley staring at me for like, the whole period of class and I even shouted to the most popular girl in our school, what was happening to me?

I closed my eyes and fell deep down to the darkness as my eyes spun faster and faster…

Into my weird dream world…

A New Visitor

"I guess you have been very tired from school, eh? I think you are tired because today was the first day of school right after the vacation." My math tutor, Vanessa stared at my face, a little worried.

"Um no, I am all right. Too many thoughts are gathering around my head. I just...argh!"

Vanessa chuckled to herself. "Haha, no need to explain, Adela. Maybe we'll finish 30 minutes earlier, so you can take a rest for a while. But I will give you a little more math homework. Deal?"

My head lit up and my eyes got bigger. "Oh my god!" I exclaimed. "Oh my god, thank you!"

"Sure," She said smiling proudly. "Now, how was the homework I gave you last time?"

I took out my notebook from my drawer and my books. "Here you go." I handed her the books and smiled.

She scanned through them and her eyes got bigger.

"Ooh! You surely did a great job, Adela. I should tell your great father that you are such a good student!"

I had a good time forgetting my headache. My teacher Vanessa was dealing with me very well I think. We finished the lesson very easily and as the time flew and pointed 5:30, Vanessa stood up and packed her things.

"You know, I have been teaching many princesses, princes or other nobles, but I think you are the best compared to other of my students!"

I grinned hardly grabbing my forehead, "Thanks a lot. That means a lot to me."

Vanessa tapped my shoulder gently and I could see her blue eyes twinkle in sunlight.

I always wanted my eyes to be blue, just like humans, but I am an Aian, so my green eyes could not possibly be blue like Vanessa's.

I stared at her eyes for a long time until she finally headed to the door waving her hand goodbye.

"Okay then, see you on next Wednesday!" she closed the door and I could still hear her footsteps down the stairs getting away from me.

I glanced at the clock which was pointing 5:30 p.m.. I needed to get ready for the ballet class.

I went toward my dressing room and got dressed in my grey tights and long blue t-shirt which I usually wear when I learn ballet. Then I went downstairs hurriedly while I tied my silky long brunette hair with my hair band. My ballet teacher, Ms. Davis was already waiting for me in the ballet room as she stretched her body. She was practicing her ballet performance that she was about to perform in front of the stage of the Broad Hall with her ballet group called 'The Swans'.

"Hello Princess Monette! Oh, don't worry, your highness. You are never late. I was just practicing my performance. Now, shall we get started?"

I trotted across the floor and stood in front of Ms. Davis, leaving a huge space between us.

Ballet is not that boring I guess. It is very fun to attend ballet class with Ms. Davis. She loves to tell stories to me about everything that she experienced last week. I always listen to her sayings carefully because I don't really have an opportunity to go travel around Anastelon except when I go to school.

"I was at the theater on Thursday last week and I performed with my group on the stage." Ms. Davis again started the conversation as we danced ballet across the floor. Then she suddenly blushed crimson. "I was being a little careless because, uh well, ballet is the thing that I always do."

I got curious and my eyes got widened. "So what happened?" I asked as I stretched out my left foot toward my head.

She giggled to herself and said, "I accidently dropped my white feather headband that I wore during that show. Some rude people laughed and most people did not, thank goodness, as I pretended that it did not happen ever so. I forgot about the headband as I concentrated on my ballet dancing and I was about to go home, just leaving my headband on the front stage."

Ms. Davis's cheeks got more crimson like her whole face was burning. She continued her stories.

"I was about to leave the Broad Hall and suddenly, someone appeared behind the wooden pillar. It was a tall man with brown long coat and I could not see his face."

"Oh my god, did you get mobbed or something?" I interrupted. I was a little frightened because the story got scarier and scarier. However, Ms, Davis laughed and shook her head gently.

"No, fortunately no, I did not get mobbed or get hurt or anything. He stood right in front of me and handed me the headband I totally forgot about! I did not have any idea at first, but I started to realize that he was a good man and he was here to give me the headband."

"Ahhh," I smiled in relief. "That is great! Did you get to know him?"

"Yes, his name was Luke and he was very kind. He even gave me a ride home and he said he wants to meet me in the café tomorrow afternoon, isn't that great?"

I looked at her a bit worriedly. "Um, are you sure that he is safe and good-minded? I mean, he could hurt you or something.

"Of course I'm sure he is kind as an angel! He even smiled at me a lot as we chatted in the car on my way home. I don't know, but when I talked to him, I felt like, I was drawn into him, like he was the Hoover and I was the dust. You know what I am saying?"

I squinted my eyes and shrugged.

"Yeah, well I am still not sure. Maybe I would know when I meet him for real."

Ms. Davis smiled as she glanced at the clock hanging on the wall. It was almost 6:30 and we had 15 more minutes left.

I stared back at Ms. Davis as I lifted my toes up and down.

"So, you are in love." I emphasized the word to make the conversation more fun.

Ms. Davis smiled even wider and answered right away. "Yes."

My eyes and my mouth got bigger. I could not speak a word for a few minutes. I finally opened my mouth.

"Then go for it! This is a good chance! I mean you were always worrying about finding your true love! This is great. You should try to draw him into you, so he will love you too! That would make a wonderful couple."

"I know, I am already planning to. He is perfect I think. He is even handsome and tall. I would not be sure that he is perfect in any way, but I would have to figure out in the café as I talk to him."

"Ask him to go to the movie theater together! Make a date, so you guys can spend more time together."

We giggled and imagined the date that Ms. Davis and that Luke guy will have tomorrow afternoon. Ms. Davis seemed as happy as she imagined how it was going to be with her first crush Luke.

Time flew until Ms. Davis suddenly looked at me in curiousness.

She asked, "How are you going to find your real love, Adela?"

I stopped me from imagining and glanced back at Ms. Davis. "Uh, I don't like any boys. Actually, I have never had someone I like before."

"How about that guy, your friend called Lowell? He seemed a little shy and cute. He's quite a gentleman, isn't he?"

I shrugged. "Well yes, he is very nice and smart, but he is just my best friend, no more than that…oh, I need to go eat my dinner. See you, Ms.

Davis!"

"Good bye Adela darling." She waved me good bye and I went upstairs to get changed into my fancy dress. I changed into my beautiful purple dress and met Brianna coming out of the guestroom. Is someone going to come to our castle? I wanted to ask.

Brianna saw me and she curtsied. "Miss Adela, King Jones and his prince Jones junior are going to come as guests and have dinner together. Please would you wear more proper clothes and tidy up your hair? Shall I make up your hair for you miss?"

I smiled and answered. "No thank you Brianna. I will make myself ready."

I was sitting on my chair right in front of Jones junior the prince from other country near Anastelon and I could not move or breathe. He was staring at me time to time as he cut his steak and put the pieces into his mouth. My moves were so unnatural and I could barely move my jaws up and down.

I did not expect myself to be in this kind of tension, until I entered the dining room and saw Jones junior; The Jones junior. I saw his blonde hair sparkle in the lights and his green eyes were piercing directly at my eyes. His smile was wonderful like the taste of honey dip and he had the perfect dimples on each of his cheek. He was just gorgeous.

I swallowed and walked inside and vowed at my mother and father. Then, I sat in front of Jones junior and he smiled at me, showing his clean arranged teeth.

"Adela dear," My mother finally spoke.

I glanced at my mother and answered. "Yes mother."

Mother smiled and looked at Charles and me.

"This young gentleman sitting in front of you is Jones junior from Elsmiere. Right next to him is your father's old friend, the King of Elsmiere, Jones. They are our guests for tonight.

"Hello Miss Monette," King Jones started to talk to me. "It is a pleasure to meet you."

"It is a pleasure to meet you, too, sir." I smiled brightly and said clearly. King Jones put his steak piece into his big mouth and said to my father. "Why, Adela looks more beautiful than she was in her childhood. She is more grown-up now."

My father chuckled as he swirled his glass or wine. "Yeah, she is almost an adult. She will be when she passes her birthday this year."

"Goodness," King Jones looked surprised and exclaimed, "My son became an adult last year."

My mother leaned against the table and smiled gently to the King Jones. "That's very nice! He would have learned everything now then. Did he graduate school last year?"

"Of course," King Jones sneered proudly, tapping Jones junior's shoulder. I swallowed my last piece of meat and quietly put down my knife and fork. Then I lifted up the cloth and tapped my lips with it.

King Jones added, "My son has overcame many exams and he never missed any perfect score on each of them. He was the best on fighter skills as well."

The door opened and the waiters came out holding the plates, of my favorite chocolate mousse. I screamed inside and slowly held my spoon up.

As the plate landed in front of me, I dug the mousse and lifted up a huge spoonful of the mousse, but I suddenly stopped. I could not show my appetite to a lovely prince sitting right in front of me. I put my spoon down on the plate of the mousse and left some mousse out of the spoon and licked it.

And it was just so delicious! The sweet and soft chocolate melted on my tongue and ran down my throat. Mmmm, I loved it so much. I had another spoon of the mousse and we all finished our dinner.

"Thank you for such a wonderful dinner King Monette. My son and I really appreciated it."

King Jones licked the spoon contently. My father stood up.

"You are very welcome, my friend. Michael, would you usher King Jones up to the deluxe room please? And Adela, would you bring Prince Jones up to his room? His room is very close to yours."

Oh my god, his room is close to my room? I have no idea why my father decided that, but it made my cheeks go red.

I stared at Prince Jones. He seemed that he wanted to hear my answer, so I blinked and finally opened my mouth. "Please follow me, Prince Jones."

I walked slowly at first down the hall, and I could hear echoing footsteps of Charles right behind me. I walked a little faster and his footsteps got faster. My heart pounded in the same tempo with his footsteps. My heart was ringing inside me and I wondered if he could hear my heart beating for him.

As I was imagining to myself, I arrived in front of Charles' guestroom that was three doors away from my room. I looked back at him and I smiled at him kindly.

"Here's your room. The bell is right beside the bed, so if you need any help, you can ring the…"

"Your name is Adela, right?" He interrupted. I got a little frightened of his interruption, but I calmed myself and answered politely.

"Yes and your name is Jones junior, I heard."

"Just call me Charles and please do not put 'junior' when you are calling my name. It kind of distracts me."

I was surprised at the way he talks so freely. My head went blank and I did not have the courage to speak. The atmosphere got awkward between me and Charles.

Charles lifted his head up and spoke hardly. "Do you want to help me arrange my stuff?"

I was glad he finally spoke. I sighed in relief and nodded. He held his key up and unlocked the door.

The guestroom was very neat and it smelled like soap and wood. The bed was completely white and the blanket and the pillows were in the closet. I closed the door behind me and saw Charles opening the closet.

I walked and stood beside him and opened the baggage. I helped him hang the clothes on to the hangers. I wanted to get rid of the awkwardness so I started speaking.

"How much did it take to come here?" I asked nervously.

He thought for a moment and said, "Well, about 1 and a half day by carriage. It would have taken less time by cars, but we had to get passed Devina and their country does not have cars, so my father decided that they would be frightened to see a car."

I giggled and stared at Charles. "How is Anastelon different to your country?"

He answered. "It is not that different, but in our country, people love to have flowers in their garden, so Elsmiere is also called as 'Country in Bloom' as a nickname."

"Oh, that is nice. I'd love to visit your country. I guess your whole country would smell like flowers." I smiled at him gently and I could feel my anxiety disappear. I was getting to know him more and more as I talked to him hanging his clothes in the closet.

After our work was done, it was almost 8:00 and I had to go to my basketball class at 8:30, so I had about 25 minutes left.

"Phew, now we're done. Do you want a cup of honey tea from Elsmiere? I brought it from my country and it is made from our flowers in Elsmiere.

I guarantee it is very sweet and delicious."

I did not have myself thinking and I answered him right away. "Yes please, that would be great."

"Ha ha yeah, I brought it just for you."

A minute later, he brought two cups of tea from the kitchen. We sat down on the chairs and I sipped the tea.

It tasted so sweet and savory. It smelled just like flowers and syrup. It was the best tea I have ever tasted.

"Oh my goodness," I exclaimed. "This is so good. I have never tasted such tea like this before! It is brilliant."

"Thank you very much. That is the reason why I brought some honey teabags from Elsmiere. I can give you some if you want."

He handed me a handful of teabags and I received them. He chuckled to himself in happiness.

"Thank you so much, Charles." I said silently.

I could not believe myself that we became such good friends like this quick. He was very friendly and I was good at listening to him. It seemed like we both didn't want to let go of this conversation.

However, the clock pointed 8:23 and I needed to get changed and get ready for my basketball lessons.

"I am so sorry Charles, but I have to go. I have my basketball lessons at 8:30 and I have to get changed into my P.E. gear."

I expected Charles to feel disappointed, but he smiled and stood up.

"No, not yet. Save your goodbyes for later on. I am learning basketball with you for today, Adela."

"What?" I screamed, not thinking of myself. When I let out the word I realized I was being rude and covered my mouth. My cheeks turned crimson like rose.

"I mean, I'm sorry. That was rude of me. I just…"

"Oh no, no need to be sorry," He gently chuckled in his way. "I always do that in front of my father. Well, not that 'what?' thing, but I sometimes forget my manners and say the word 'stupid' in front of my father."

I made my mouth a shape of an 'O' and stared at him wondering if he was telling the truth. He stared at me back with his big gorgeous smile on his face. I looked at the time and jumped.

"Oh my, we need to go, it's almost 8:25 and we need to get changed. Do you have appropriate clothes for fitness?" I headed to the door and shouted at him.

"Yes I have mine," He shouted back at me as he opened his closet. "From Elsmiere."

"Good. I will see you downstairs. Oh! And you should go downstairs and turn left. You will see the sign on the right."

"I've got it. Thank you so much, Adela." He shouted happily as I closed the door behind me.

I ran to my room and got changed into my P.E. gear. I tied my long hair, which comes near my hip, into a neat ponytail. I showed myself in front of a big mirror of my size and turned around. I admitted that I looked pretty in a white basketball t-shirt with black shorts. I wore my red converse high-tops and headed to the gym.

"Hey, Adela. You are late for the first time of the class." Morris was holding the basketball and had an annoyed expression on his face. He was a little strict and he was sensitive with the time.

"Sorry, I am late. By the way, Jones junior…I mean Charles is going to come as well."

"Charles? Who is he? Is he your friend or something or your boyfriend maybe?"

"No, um he is well…oh, there he comes!"

I pointed at the door as Charles came in bursting inside.

"I am terribly sorry I am late on the first class. I could not find my P.E. gear stuck in the pile. Anyway, it's nice to see you here again Adela."

"Charles, are you her boyfriend or something? I have never seen a guy with Adela before, except that guy called Lowell."

Charles turned and glanced at Morris with his gentle eyes. He said, "Hello, nice to meet you. My name is Charles and I'm her new friend."

"Well, nice to meet you too, Charles." Morris smiled showing his teeth.

"Have you ever learned basketball before?"

"Yeah sure, I always have. Wanna to play a game?"

"Sure, why not?" Morris was always like that playing games with other people and winning. I bet he lives by the joy of winning in basketball.

"Adela, you can be in Charles' team and I will do it alone." Morris dribbled the ball with his right hand and stared at both of us.

"Here we go!" Morris shouted as he passed through the space between us. Charles and I chased Morris and Charles slicked away the ball and passed it to me. So, I dribbled the way along and jumped for shooting.

Bull's eye! The ball went straight into the net.

"Good job, Adela, you are better than I thought!" Charles exclaimed as he wiped his sweat off his forehead. I breathed in and out and smiled at him.

"Thanks, but you were good, too. Actually, I did not do anything and you passed me the..."

"Okay, okay no more love chitchats," Morris squeaked his voice annoyingly as he picked up the ball. "Gym is for competitions and sports. Now, I will teach you both more complex techniques in basketball."

"I had so much fun in basketball class." Charles was jumping up and down and drank some water from his bottle. He was hyper because he won every game with Morris. "I liked that Morris guy. He has a taste in sports."

I laughed at him and looked at him if he was joking.

"Haha, you're joking aren't you? I am always annoyed by him whenever he scolds me. He is too strict, but now I am used to his classes."

"See? That's how you learn sports. You get easily used to it because this is how the sports should be like and I think he knows the right way of sports." Charles looked at me as we arrived in front of my room. He stared at me closely as I opened the door with my key. I opened the door and stared at him.

"Well, I need to go now, good bye!" I turned around and stepped inside.

Suddenly, I felt his warm hand touch my shoulder. My heart jumped.

Oh my god, he had his hand on my shoulder. I looked around.

He was about to say something, but he hesitated and smiled to himself. He finally opened his mouth.

"I was just wondering…who is this Lowell guy that Morris mentioned? Is he your…um… boyfriend maybe?"

My heart was pounding faster and louder as I felt the warmness on my shoulder.

I finally found myself and chewed my lips.

"Oh, um…I am not sure I should tell you or not." I stepped inside my room and waved him good bye. But he wanted to know the answer.

"But, Adela, why won't you tell me?" I heard his voice after I closed the door.

"I will tell you later." I shouted archly to him as I turned on the light. My room was very clean and I knew Brianna took care of it when I wasn't here. I breathed the air smelling like the brand new lavender soap and went to my closet. I changed into my pajamas and turned off the lights. Then I was quickly asleep.

A Walk Outside

The telephone rang. I held it up as I flipped to another page of my book called 'The Sorrows of Young Werther'. This book was the saddest book I have ever read and I was crying my eyes out of it. My eyes were already red and wet, so I wiped my tears and I hardly spoke.

"Hello?" my voice croaked.

"Hey, I am so sorry to bother you right now. Is this a bad time for me to visit your house?"

I jumped up and glanced at my clock. It was pointing at exact 4:00pm and I had so much free time for today.

"Ah," I groaned and answered. "Um sure. I have a lot of free time today."

"Great. Will you let me enter?"

"Okay. Wait a minute."

I put down the phone and my book. I spoke through the microphone that goes to the maids' room and called out. "Guys, please open the door for my friend Catherine and let her in."

I grabbed my book and grabbed the microphone again.

"Oh, and bring her to the back garden. Prepare two cups of black tea."

I was holding my book: 'The Sorrows of Young Werther' as I went down the stairs. When I finally arrived at the first floor, I turned right.

However, I bumped into something that felt soft and cozy and I dropped my book simultaneously.

I stepped back and thought I had bumped into a maid. It was Charles, wearing his white shirt and his black formal pants and shoes. He looked stunned and hesitated.

My mouth made a shape of an 'O' and looked down.

"Oh my goodness, I am so sorry Charles, I was being so clumsy and in a hurry. Are you okay?"

"Uh, yeah I am all right."

Charles blushed scarlet as I looked through his eyes. He smiled and picked my book up and glanced at it.

"Hmm, 'The Sorrows of Young Werther' you're reading? This was a nice and sentimental book I recall. Do you like it?"

"Yes," I smiled back at him. "This book is just beautiful. It is about this young man called Werther dying because a woman called Lotte could not marry him. I liked the way Werther writes to his friend as he watches Lotte with his heart."

Charles riffled through the book until he reached the pages that I dropped my tears on. Those pages were wet and bended. Charles looked up.

"Do you cry a lot when you read these sad books?" He asked curiously.

I grinned and touched the wet pages that I cried on. "Yes as you can see, I always cry when reading these sad romantic books that my mother buys me. But they are all fun to read."

I glanced at the backdoor that leads to the garden. Michael was waving at me to come quickly. I completely have forgotten about Cathy.

"Oh, I need to go quick. I will see you later." I took a last glance at Charles and swished to the backdoor. I ran to the garden and saw Cathy shouting at the maids.

"I want my friend in here all right? I have waited for 15 minutes and she is still not...hey!"

Cathy saw me and ran into me. "I was just talking to your maids right now to bring you here because I have waited for such a long time." She seemed less angry than before.

"No. It is my fault. I bumped into Charles and I talked with him for a while."

"Charles?" Her eyes got bigger. "Who is he? Is he your new boyfriend?"

"No. He is a new visitor, from Elsmiere."

"Elsmiere...you mean that country with a lot of flower gardens and sort of things like that? I saw that picture in the magazine! It is the place I've always wanted to travel to."

"Oh, so have I. He gave me all those honey teabags from his country. It tasted so nice."

I could see that Cathy was very curious about Charles. Then she clicked her fingers and pulled my arm.

"Come on," she winked and pulled. "I am so tired of visiting your castle all the time and sitting on this dumb chair. Let's go somewhere different."

I thought for a moment. "Then where do you want to go?"

She grinned excitedly. "Outside the castle for freedom."

Cathy pulled me to my parents' conference room where my father and mother read letters from the people and discuss the law. I was not allowed to talk to them when they are in their works. However, Cathy did not know.

"Cathy, I am so sorry my father and mother are in the conference room and I can't go inside whenever I want. It is the rule in here." I whispered worriedly to Cathy as she bit her lips, trying to figure out what to do.

"When are they going to finish their work then?" She asked quietly.

"Um, I need to ask that as well, so it is not a good time to ask them for permission. Also, I have rarely gone out of the castle for fun, either."

Cathy was not listening to me. She was asking a maid beside the door when I looked behind at her.

"Excuse me, may I ask when the majesties are going to finish their work? It is kind of urgent."

The maid thought for a minute and quietly knocked the door. Then she went inside and whispered in my mother's ear. My mother glanced out the door and quickly and quietly whispered back to the maid.

The maid hurriedly came out and smiled at us.

"Her majesty says it'll take 3 hours." The maid quietly walked away as she finished her speech. Cathy looked back at me.

"This is the chance! You can get back in three hours and pretend you did not go anywhere. That would be perfect."

I hesitated for a while and I nodded. "That is not a bad idea. Let's go! We can travel around Anastelon and play together."

But, there was a problem for me. I should not let my face out or a lot of people would try to see the princess of Anastelon. I needed something to hide my face.

"Here, use this to hide your face. I brought my sunglasses from my house. Put the cap on." Cathy dressed me up simply. I looked at myself in the mirror and I stood out too much.

"Cathy," I called her worriedly. "I appreciate you are trying to hide my face and make people not recognize me, but don't you think these clothes make me stand out too much?"

Cathy thought to herself and shook her head.

"Nope, you're perfectly safe. I know it."

Cathy and I sneaked out of the castle and out of the gate. Then, we were free by ourselves. Cathy and I were so excited that we jumped up and down together.

"Oh my god, I mean really Adel. Your parents really should let you out frequently. How could a princess do not know about how Anastelon looks like?"

I was not listening to Cathy's complaints. I looked around a beautiful country Anastelon. There were many people and also small cute kids walking by with their parents. Small buildings up to about five floors located closely together and cars swished through the roads. I was not able to see Anastelon this specifically when I rode a limousine to school. It was just beautiful and peaceful.

"Come on," Cathy pulled my arm. "Let's go to 'Muffin Divers'."

We arrived at this café and the wooden sign was written as 'Muffin Divers' with pictures of muffins, cakes and coffee. We went inside and sat in the table beside the wall.

Cathy was so excited and hyper. "You haven't ever been here right? I can recommend you some delicious muffins and drinks. I always come here to do my homework because it's quiet in here and I love their muffins too! They are so scrumptious and sweet. I always choose to eat chocolate muffins whenever I come here. Blueberry is good too. What do you want?"

I shrugged and stared at Cathy. "I will have the same thing you choose."

Cathy giggled and stood up. "Let me choose first then, I am going to order blueberry today. You will love these muffins, I swear. Want coffee?"

I looked up at her and nodded gently. Cathy ran to the counter and ordered the food. I looked around table to table and saw many people in the café. There were children, couples, families and even old people were sitting down with smiles on their faces.

Then, I saw someone that made my heart stop. My eyes got bigger and I stopped breathing.

It was Vanessa, sitting as she faced a tall skinny man in front of her. Vanessa was just only two tables away and I could see her so close. But she did not notice me yet. The man must be Luke, I thought when Cathy sat in front of me holding the plates and cups.

"Here's yours and here's mine," Cathy grabbed her muffin and took a big bite.

"Come on Adela, taste it. It's really good."

I bit into the muffins slowly and chewed. The muffin was very delicious just like Cathy told me. Inside it was fresh minced blueberries that were very chewy. I finished my muffin and started drinking the coffee. I kept staring at Vanessa though.

Cathy followed my glimpse and looked back at me. "Who are you looking at?"

I murmured. "Uh, you see that young woman with ginger ponytail? That is my ballet teacher, Vanessa."

"Oh, so what's the deal about her?" Cathy could not understand, so I explained everything to her briefly about what Vanessa and I talked about in ballet class. Cathy was into the story about her.

"Ah, so she is in love." Cathy grinned as she joked.

I laughed very hard at her expressions. "Haha, that was what I said when Vanessa told me about that!"

"So, you are spying on her?" Cathy asked curiously.

"Yeah, I am somehow trying to help Vanessa get a boyfriend. Oh, they stood up from their seats! Look!"

Vanessa and Luke stood up. Luke led her out of the café and we could see they were holding hands together. Luke was pointing at the movie theater across the streets and Vanessa was giggling.

Cathy laughed softly. "Wow, they look so happy together. I mean they are even holding hands, which probably means they are going out with each other!"

I smiled and I was in relief that she finally found her love. I suddenly remembered the book that I brought with me.

"Oh, and I forgot. Do you know the book called 'The Sorrows of Young Werther'? I brought it here."

"No I haven't heard of it before, but it looks like a fun book. What genre?"

"It is Sentimental Romance." I told her.

"Can I borrow it?" She hugged the book like she did not want to let it go. "Can I please borrow it? I will return it soon."

I could not deny her. "Okay alright. I will let you borrow this book."

Cathy was in delight that she borrowed a book of romance from me and ate her favorite muffin. She was happy that she was out with her best friend and spying on a teacher. We had so much fun together.

After our fun times, I had to go back to my house and Cathy walked together for me to my gate. Then, my cell phone rang.

I held it up. Lowell was calling and I received it.

"Hello?"

"Hey Adela," Lowell shouted happily through the phone.

"I told you a week ago that I will visit your house today. Am I able to?"

I looked at the time and smiled. "Yeah sure, of course, when are you coming?"

"I'm coming right now. I will call Cathy to come as well."

"Cathy is here with me, so just come along."

"Okay great, see you later."

"Bye Lowell."

I put my phone in my jacket and Cathy was jumping up and down in excitement.

"Oh my goodness, Lowell is coming? I need to see him, can I stay?"

I shrugged. "Well, as long as your parents let you stay outside for a long time, you can."

"I can't miss seeing Lowell for heaven's sake! You know I love him more than anything else."

Cathy was always anxious to see Lowell, even at school. She tidied her blonde hair and smiled prettily.

"How do I look?" Cathy asked as she made all kinds of facial expression she could make.

I grinned at her and held my thumb up. "You look awesome, don't worry."

Lowell arrived 20 minutes later and Cathy and I were in my bedroom chatting.

"Your highness, Mr. Henderson has arrived." Michael called out through the interphone.

I jumped up and grabbed the microphone. "Get him in and usher him to my room please."

Cathy's face was lightened up. "He is here already? Geez"

A minute later, somebody knocked outside the door. I opened and there was Lowell standing outside the door.

"Hey Adela, where's Cathy?" He smiled and stepped inside. Cathy stood up from my bed and smiled at him as kindly as she could.

"Hi Lowell," Cathy waved at him and smiled shyly. Lowell also glanced at her and smiled with his gorgeous dimple. Then he walked to the sofa and sat down while Cathy giggled quietly to herself in excitement. Cathy and I came along and sat in front of Lowell, who was closing his eyes and pretending that he was asleep.

Cathy stared at Lowell and grinned. "Lowell, you don't look good. Actually, you look kind of pale and weary."

I agreed with Cathy. "Yeah, you look sleepy for sure. What happened to you?"

Lowell opened his eyes and stood up from his seat and looked at us half-waken.

"Yeah, actually I am. I think it's all because of these choosing my classes and attending all of them that I have my interests on. They are making me crazy since the first day of the class."

"What classes did you choose Lowell?" Cathy asked Lowell curiously.

Lowell counted with his fingers. "Um, I am interested in Geography and Science, so I chose those two classes. Plus, I thought I may need to improve my math grade, so I chose Math and I also chose Literature and Geology and…"

"Whoa whoa, hold it over there," I was stunned that he was making so many classes than I expected.

Well, maybe it was normal for him to be like that. He is a straight A student and he is even better than me, so he sometimes teaches me and Cathy.

I sighed. "You are way too far out for yourself. I mean, look. You chose 7 or 8 classes a day. How are you supposed to manage while doing other things? Also, we just finished our vacation. We need some time to get used to our school routine by starting off easy."

Cathy stared at Lowell, looking worried and sad. "Yes, and we are all in our last year of university and you have worked so hard over the last three years. Don't be so greedy of yourself."

Lowell sighed and murmured, "I know, I still am regretting. But, I can't cancel them can I? I already took the first classes."

"Just ask the office lady. I know her really well and I think she is friendly. She may help you out."

"I think I should. Hey Adela, you want to hang out with me tonight? We can go to the 'Muffin Divers' together. You may not know, they have the best muffin…"

"I already took her there." Cathy interrupted. Lowell thought for a long time and clicked his fingers.

"Hey, you know what? Why don't we go to the movies? They have the best movies recently. You know 'King's Army'?"

"Yeah," Cathy jumped up from her seat. "I heard that movie made a hit on the first week right after it came out! Please Adela please can we go?"

I shrugged and thought to myself. Actually tonight, our family was about to have a family meeting. I was not sure I can miss that meeting which my father thought it important.

"I am not sure about that. Our family will have a family meeting after dinner and now it is like 6:30pm. We don't have much time."

Lowell became upset and sad. "Then what are we going to do? I came here to hang out with you and you are telling me to go now, aren't you?"

"Why don't we go together this time, Lowell?" Cathy pleaded. "You went with Adela the last time, so maybe...?"

Lowell hesitated for a second. His eyes shifted nervously. "Well, um sorry Cathy, maybe next time."

Cathy's smile disappeared. I glared at Lowell. Why is he always so closed-minded with Cathy? I thought. I had to think of a way.

I thought for a minute. "Maybe we can have dinner together. Wait for me outside and I will change myself into my dress."

Unexpected

I came outside of my closet wearing a blue shiny dress and a pearl necklace. I tied up my hair neatly and went outside.

Lowell was chatting with Cathy and they stopped and glanced at me.

"Wow," Cathy smiled and opened her mouth. "You are ever so pretty whenever you wear your dress. I think you are born to be a princess."

I grinned shyly and looked at Lowell. Lowell did not speak a word. He just stared at me up and down. When he realized that I was staring at him, he murmured softly. "Wonderful," he said.

We walked down the stairs and went to the dining room where my mother and father were sitting and silently waiting. My mother seemed surprised at my friends, but she later smiled at us.

"Come inside my dears," My mother said softly. "Make yourself at home."

My friends and I sat down close to each other. Lowell sat right beside me and Cathy seemed like she wanted to sit next to Lowell.

"Cathy, do you want to sit here instead?"

My mother looked up suddenly and said. "Oh, Adela. Would you please sit where you were allocated?"

I sat down on my chair and Cathy had to sit next to my mother. I felt sorry for Cathy for making her stay away from Lowell, but I could not help it.

"Sorry we were late," King Jones and Charles came inside the dining room apologizing to us. Charles glanced at me and smiled, then looked at everyone else. Then he stared at Lowell and his face hardened. He seemed like he wanted to say something, but he seemed to try not to. Losing his smile, he just stared at his plate.

"Here is our dinner." My father said happily. The chef brought us mushroom soup as appetizers. I did not eat it much. Not because it was not delicious or I was not hungry, I was staring at Charles the whole time.

I did not know why he was looking so scared or frightened. Maybe he forgot some things, or he made a mistake, I thought. But why would his smile disappear at the time he glanced at Lowell's face?

It was such a mystery. I tried to think of a way. Maybe he knew Lowell and they were rivals. Nah, that is not really possible. Hmm, then what did he feel frightened at? I really wanted to ask him. Also, Charles seemed like he wanted to say something. However, we both couldn't because my mother would say like, "Adela, how rude! Do not talk while eating."

I stopped thinking about it. It was confusing and it got me a headache. He would tell me after dinner, period.

After dinner we stood up from our seat and Cathy and Lowell seemed to be heading home. However, my mother grabbed both of them and whispered in their ears.

'I am sorry I keep you here for so long, but we need you for the family meeting.'

Lowell, Cathy and I all went to the meeting room and sit around a small wooden table. Charles sat next to me and Cathy got to sit with Lowell this time. My father stood up and started talking as everyone sat down.

"Good evening and welcome to our family meeting." He started and coughed before he spoke again. "We have something very important to say in this meeting, where we all gather. Brianna, would you bring that please?"

Brianna came in and handed over a book to my father. Then she went out and closed the door behind her.

"In the law manual of Anastelon, when a princess or a prince becomes 18 years old, he or she should have a special ceremony before he or she becomes a king or queen of this kingdom."

I gasped. "I beg your pardon," I said quietly. "So you are talking about me becoming 18 and having a ceremony before I become a queen?"

"Yes, that's right." He answered promptly. "Specifically, the ceremony I mean here is the process of becoming a strong, broad-minded and having many experiences."

"I still don't get it, father." I interrupted.

What does he want me to do?

"As a member of this kingdom, you, Adela, should walk all the way to your Aunt's country and get the sacred jewel. The jewel is what you will need as to receive the throne after us. The rule is that you can take an expert and 2 more people."

I thought for a second. "I've got it. I will take Lowell and Catherine. But who is the expert?"

I looked around and caught Charles' eye. Oh my god, I knew it right away. He was the expert that my father was talking about. He was coming with me on the travel.

"Oh my god," I murmured by accident. My father squinted at me, but continued.

"Anyway, the ceremony will start tomorrow."

"Tomorrow?" I shrieked. "That fast? I mean, I did not even pack my stuff yet, nor I am ready for it!"

"You can pack your goods tonight and you can get ready on your travel. Mr. Jones junior will teach you how to deal with danger." My mother said gently.

"Adela, there's one more rule," My father added. "You should travel through these three countries, which are Devina, Elsmiere, Lanya and there's actually one more kingdom called Vulgary clan where the evil stays. You will get more information on your way to Aragon. So all of you are taking this path along to achieve a mission of getting the jewel, and this whole process is what we call the 'Quest'."

I calmed myself down and took deep breaths. There was no way that I could go through that many countries and one evil devastating clan called Vulgary.

Vulgary was the clan that has a history of 1000 years. That clan is full of dirty stuff, I once read in the library. They are very strong that they almost destroyed my aunt's country, Aragon. Fortunately, we helped them out fighting against them and they were able to fix their kingdom again. After that until today, Vulgary has closed its gates and no one knows what's happening inside.

I could find many eyes staring upon me. That time I found out that I was standing from my seat and punching the table. I sat down and murmured. "Humph!"

Charles chuckled. "Well, if Adela doesn't like me to go with her, I will allow her to choose other great experts."

I was about to say something, but my mother interrupted.

"No, that won't be allowable for you to choose my dear Prince Jones. I am sorry to say Adela, that it is the rule."

I hesitated and thought for a minute. Then, I finally opened my mouth.

"Uh well, if my mother and father want me to do it, I will go for it then."

Catherine and Lowell looked a little worried. "What about our school?" Lowell said to my mother. Cathy also said loudly to my parents. "Yeah, I mean we would love to go on a trip to Aragon with Adela, but we have our school works to do, and actually, Lowell has his huge schedule to go to the best university."

"No hold on Cathy," Lowell interrupted. Lowell seemed to consider a lot between the country's law and his schoolwork. I knew it was so hard to choose between both of them because he has been preparing to go to the most prestigious school in Anastelon. I wondered what he would choose. Minutes later, he sighed and finally opened his mouth.

"Your majesty, I will go with the princess. I will take the quest with her."

Everyone sighed in relief. Cathy stood up and said loudly to my mother.

"I will go with Adela too." Cathy looked at me and smiled.

"All right then," My mother smiled big as she could. "Prepare for the quest tonight. Catherine and Lowell, you may come to our palace at exactly 6:00 tomorrow morning. The ceremony will be held at that time and you should not be late for it!"

Preparing for Tomorrow

My mother ended the family meeting. I went out to usher my friends out of the palace. Cathy asked a maid to usher her to the bathroom and the maid took her. Lowell and I stood awkwardly outside the door and our eyes met.

I sighed. "I knew you are putting much effort into preparation of going to such prestigious university in our country, but I just wanted to ask you." I stood close to Lowell. "Why didn't you say no to my mother?"

Lowell did not say anything and stood still. I knew he was still suffering inside between his effort and an order. However, he did not answer me.

"You could have denied her offer. We are friends, remember? It may sound like such a huge order, but it is always up to you. My mother would have still appreciated your opinion even if you said no to her."

Lowell still did not say anything. He hung his head down and I knew he almost cried. I could see his mouth open and he finally spoke.

"Adela," He did not sob. He murmured in sadness. He suddenly stepped into me and covered his arm around me. Ah, I did not know what to do or say in that moment, so I stood there feeling his emotion.

"Adela," He called me again. "Have you ever felt the feeling when you are about to lose what you have prepared for your entire life? Do you know that kind of feeling?"

I wrapped my arms around his back. I felt his soft chest and his heartbeat.

"I had to choose between my whole life effort and friendship. It was so hard for me. It was…"

"No need to explain, Lowell," I looked into his eyes, still having my arms around him. "I fully understand that feeling inside you."

His eyes twinkled with something that I could not notice. He hugged me again and I hugged him back. "Thank you Lowell," I mumbled in his chest. "Thank you for coming with me to the quest. You are such a good friend to me."

Suddenly, I could hear a few footsteps and Lowell and I came apart and stood a little away from each other. We could hear Cathy mumbling to herself.

"Oh, why isn't the toilet flushing? It would not have taken a long time for me to…"

She stopped talking as she found us beside the door. "Oh, hey. What were you two doing?"

"Nothing," Lowell answered for me. "Let's go, Cathy."

I walked to my room and found Charles standing in front of my door waiting for me. I was confused about it and walked close to him and asked.

"What are you doing in front of my door may I ask?"

"I was waiting for you," Charles answered. "I wanted to ask you something."

I grinned in confusion. "Wh...What would you ask?"

He stepped close to me. "I wanted to ask you, who is the guy called Lowell?"

I stared at him for a minute. Now I remembered his reaction when he saw Lowell in the dining room. He was shocked to meet him face to face. Oh, and I remembered the moment when Morris said he had never seen a guy beside me except Lowell. Oh my god, I think he caught his words that moment.

I laughed and squinted at him. "Why would you want to know?"

"Because I have rights to know about you."

"But we just became friends," I teased him. "Why should I trust you?"

"Oh, come on, please Adela," He was now begging me. "Tell me who that guy is."

"Okay fine, he is just my friend. And there's nothing more than that."

Charles seemed to not trust me at all. "Are you sure?"

"Yup," I nodded smiling. "Lowell, Cathy and I are best friends since kindergarten. We love each other as friends. "

Charles seemed relieved. I did not know why he had to care about that. It was a little weird for me.

"Okay then, I will see you tomorrow Adel. Good night."

"Good night." He waved at me and closed his door. I hesitated and called him again.

"Charles?"

His door opened in a second. He stared at me and answered in his sweet lovely voice. "Yes ma'am?"

"I want you to bring some honey teabags for the quest."

I could see his eyes getting bigger and he smiled with a cute dimple. He nodded with his handsome grin. "Sure, I will see you tomorrow."

"Good night, Charles." I closed the door behind me and turned on the lights. Then I walked toward the dressing room and got changed into my pajamas. I lay down on my soft bed. The bed sheet smelled like lilac and it reminded me of two things.

First, today was the day that Brianna changed my bed sheet into a cleaner one. I bet she had used the detergent which has a scent of lilac. It was my favorite since I was five. I remember I always begged Brie to use the lilac detergent for me and she started to use only that kind. It gave me that bloomy feeling when I lay down on my bed right now.

Second, it reminded me of Charles. I closed my eyes and started to draw his face on a piece of paper in my imagination. He had sparkling chocolate eyes with silky blonde hair which was a little darker than sunlight. I imagined his room and the moment I helped him put his clothes into the closet. And after that, he showed me his honey teabags from Elsmiere and I can see myself excited. I caught his word saying, 'I brought it just for you.'

He brought it just for me? I was confused. He brought his teabags for me. Why was I thinking of his words over and over?

I opened my eyes and stopped my confusing imagination. I could see my dark room around me. I closed my eyes again and went to sleep.

The Quest

The alarm rang at exactly at 4 in the morning. I woke up and took out my suitcase from the closet. When I was finding clothes and putting them inside my suitcase, Brianna appeared and she ran over to me.

"Your highness, I just heard a rule that a princess should have only a small bag with some water and extra clothes. I brought a bottle filled with water and…oh no, your highness, that suitcase is not allowable for you to take on your quest."

My mouth made a shape like an 'o'. "What?" I shrieked. "My father is not allowing me to take all the clean clothes? But, I can get dirty in a few days and if I take only these, I will get dirtier and dirtier."

Brianna could not say anything. I thought she had the same opinion with me, but she refuted. "To tell the truth, I think the same, but miss, your father says that in travelling, it is more comfortable to bring a small bag with you or else it would take a long time getting there and back to Anastelon."

I sighed and put my suitcase back to the closet and brought out a small bag from it and packed again. When I finished packing and getting dressed, the doorbell rang. I opened and saw Charles in his comfortable clothes and a bag. It was my first time seeing him in his comfortable normal clothes. He always wore his formal suit as a prince. I wore my normal clothes only when I went to school.

"Hey, Adela," He called me as he saw my door open. He stared at me head to toe and smiled.

"You look pretty today." He looked a little more nervous and tense than usual. I thought it was because of the quest that he was going to have with me. I blushed and looked down at my clothes and grinned.

"Well, I thought they are too normal and informal for me. I am glad you like them."

"I think you are always beautiful in every clothes you wear."

That made my heart beat loudly. I smiled awkwardly at him. "Thanks, I like your style, too."

I went downstairs with Charles and I was breathing in and out until I arrived in front of the door of our castle. There were Anastelonians waiting behind the gate, hanging onto the metal door. Everyone was waving their flag of Anastelon and staring at me. They shouted, "Safe quest for Princess Adela Beth Monette!" as they screamed in delight. I stepped across the carpet and stood with Charles.

I breathed in and out. Gosh, why was I born to be a princess? I should have become one of those Anastelonians waving the flag for a princess for her safe trip.

Charles rolled his eyes at me. He stared at my frightened face and chuckled.

"Feeling nervous?" He whispered in his low voice. I looked up at him and shook my head with my mouth shut. Charles seemed nervous too, but he was not as frightened as me.

I could hear some banging and screaming cheers from outside of the castle. What was happening? I wondered in confusion. There were some loud cheers and colorful cars with loud music and drums. I bet my mother told the circus troupes to prepare a huge parade for me. There having fireworks in the morning. Great.

I sighed and calmed myself down as the gate opened slowly. The car drove inside right in front of the stairs where we were standing and Lowell and Cathy came out from the car.

The people clapped as they walked gently toward us. They were also wearing normal clothes like Charles and me. Cathy looked at me and smiled. We stood side by side close to each other.

The clock tower struck six in the morning and rang loudly. My heart pounded in the triple pace with the clock. Don't be nervous, Adela, I told myself. You are now about to start the most important part of your life. Charles, Lowell, Cathy and I, we are about to start an amazing quest.

The Beginning

We started to walk inside the forest of Anastelon. It was a fine sunny morning I supposed. I walked close to Lowell and talked with him.

"Are you okay?" I asked carefully looking at his face. He did not say anything. He was still in his shock from yesterday.

"I don't know." Lowell bit his lip with a soft smile. He did not feel alright.

"Aww, I am so sorry, Lowell. It's…my entire fault. I shouldn't have taken you to this quest. I should have taken other guys in school, maybe like, Jacob or Cody."

"What? Are you kidding?" He chuckled and stared at me. "No way, those guys are jerks. They don't even know you much as well. And Adela, please don't feel sorry for this. I thought about this and I came over with it. So in conclusion, friendship is more important than my grade and that is my final answer."

I smiled softly. "Thank you again, Lowell. You are such a good friend."

"Thanks," He said quietly. "I thought I deserved that."

Charles glanced at Lowell and kept staring. I thought he was looking for the time to say hi to him, but at last failed because Lowell did not even try to look at him.

Cathy took notice of his action and stopped. "Hey," She smiled brightly as if she got a good idea. "I know what we are going to do before we start this fun quest."

Everyone stopped and stared at Cathy. "What?" Lowell squinted.

"Oh my god, I can't believe the royal ceremony did not allow us to do this. We don't know each other well, so they should have made us introduce to each other."

Whoa, that was a big mistake that Cathy found from our royal ceremony. I wonder how my mother would act like if she noticed that.

Lowell did not seem pleased with her idea. "We know who we are and where we are from. So I think we can skip that part, just like it was skipped during the ceremony Cathy." He said as he glanced at Charles.

Charles caught his eye and smiled. "Well, ceremony should be completed as perfect. Let me introduce myself first. My name is Charles Peter Jones junior from Elsmiere. I am the prince of Elsmiere and our country is full of flowers."

Cathy clapped. "Yeah, I love Elsmiere. I had been there once, when I was young, and I only have good memories within it."

"Oh, really? That's very nice." Charles smiled at Cathy and stepped closer to her. "I know your name is Catherine, would you please introduce yourself?"

"Well, I haven't introduced myself much before except when I had to move school. This is such a sudden event for me, um well first, my full name is Catherine Middleton and I don't have a middle name."

Charles was surprised. He may be because I was surprised as well when

I heard her name when she told me about it. It was because royals always have middle names named after famous royals. Mine, which is Beth, was my aunt, who fought in the war with the Vulgary clan. She fought really hard, my mother claimed. She told me the story of my aunt Beth shortly. When I heard of that story, I was so impressed by her that she fought bravely in the war. So every night I begged Brianna to stay in the bed with me secretly and repeat the heroic story of my aunt Beth. Every time we were together in bed like we were doing slumber parties, she was excited and told me more about her.

"The great Miss Beth fought against hundreds of evil soldiers and killed all of them. I heard that she fought with three weapons which were a sword, a bow and arrows and the last weapon was well, I am not sure. The rumor says that there were three weapons, but no one is sure what the last one is. It says that the last weapon only existed one in the entire world."

I was shocked and gasped. I took a guess and whispered. "Maybe it was like…a magical wand. She may have killed them all using the magical wand when she was tired."

Brianna giggled and patted my head. "Maybe it was, maybe it was. Now it is too late miss. Good night." I always wondered what the last weapon would be. I believed that it would be a precious weapon and I wished to know about it. But the answer was unfound still.

When I was dreaming in my flashback, Lowell came closer to me and whispered.

"Still feeling nervous?"

Whoa, my flashback popped and I glanced at Lowell. He smiled at me with his silky blond hair swishing over to the back. I smiled back awkwardly and answered. "Nah, I had a flashback."

I stared at Charles and Cathy. They were chattering about flowers. I was surprised that they had the same interest; Charles who was from the country with many kinds of flowers and Cathy who majors Ecology."

"They are going to be great friends, aren't they?" Lowell murmured as he stared at them. We both giggled as we walked down the rocky road. I looked around and realized that we were in the deep forest.

"Hey Charles," I called. He stopped and looked back at me. "How long is the way to Devina?"

Charles thought for a moment. "I remember my father saying about it long the way to Anastelon and I thought it was...about...130 kilometers."

"Wait, what?" I gasped in horror. Oh my god I couldn't believe what he just said out loud. I have never heard of that big number before.

"That is impossible! I can't do that, Charles. It's going to take years..."

"No, it is not Miss Monette. It may take only about less than 3 days if we keep walking."

"But there are going to be more. We have to get across 3 countries to get to Aragon. It is going to be dangerous with all those demons or carnivorous hunters and stuff like that."

"Adela," Charles stared at me with his eyes full of crystals. "It is your quest. It started because of you. You can't get over your complaints. It is your authority and your dear friends and I are here to help you, not to torture you."

Then, I realized. This was my quest. This was my authority. This was what I had to accomplish to become the real adult, the real queen of Anastelon. I shouldn't be like this. Even Lowell and Cathy were giving up their school works, just for me. I turned and glanced at Lowell and Cathy, who seemed worried about me complaining.

"Guys," I grinned at them. "I am so sorry. I forgot that you guys are suffering more than me."

Cathy giggled. "Well, we are not suffering right now, because this sacrificing is for our friendship, for our most precious friend Adela."

"Yeah, and I am all ready for this trip," Lowell grinned back at me. "I want to rock n roll."

"Yes," I stepped forward looking in front of me. "Let's rock 'n' roll."

Long Way to Devina

From then, I gained power from my friends and especially Charles. He made me think of myself and the ones who are sacrificing for me. Thanks to him, we could speed up for a little bit and get rid of the awkwardness.

"Wow, I have never been to this kind of forest before," Cathy exclaimed in joy.

"Full of animals, full of trees and full of mystery. I love it! It feels like I am studying alive in my ecology class."

Lowell laughed. "Yeah Cathy, look, feel and learn. That is the best way of learning."

Cathy blushed a little. "It is good for me to see all these stuffs that are related to my studies I think."

We walked miles of the forest for hours.

I stared at Charles who was quietly looking forward. As we kept walking, we could get out of the forest for a while with the bright sunlight. The sun was shining brightly right above us.

I noticed my stomach grumble. I grabbed my stomach and murmured.

"I think it is around lunchtime. Maybe we should prepare for our lunch."

"Whoa, the first meal of our trip it is!" Charles exclaimed and sat down on the grass under the tree. "We should get ready for our meal."

"What are we going to eat?" Cathy asked. "We didn't even bring any food with us."

"We can hunt animals of course," Charles answered. "or maybe edible plants."

Ew, I groaned in disgust. But I will have to put myself into this kind of thing. This was going to continue on for a year during the trip.

"Who wants to help me hunt?" Charles asked.

"I will look for some edible plants or fruits," Cathy yelled. "I love the nature."

Lowell thought for a minute. Then he opened his mouth. "Maybe girls should look for the plants and we, the boys should hunt. That may be the safest."

Charles smiled. "Sure Lowell, come here and get the hunting equipments."

Blood...was definitely disgusting! The rabbits' meat were sizzling on the stick near the fire and around us, there were blood and the animal skin all over the grass. But I could not say anything. We all sat down in the circle and waited for the meat to be ready.

Of course, Cathy and I also got huge chunks of green edible plants such as Dandelions and Pokeweed. I did not know much about the plants, so Cathy looked for it and I had to ask her everything. In the end, Cathy found most of the edible plants and I found some raspberries and also blueberries.

The meat started to turn goldish brown and the oil started to ooze out from it. Charles gathered the oil into a small bottle and said, "We may need this oil to put on fire at night."

The meat was ready and we started eating it with our hands. I grabbed some of the raspberries from the chunk and chewed. The raspberries were juicy, sweet, and they had a strong sour taste. I felt that they were even better than the raspberries that I eat at home. Well, that was better than I thought.

Charles took a bite of the rabbit meat and chewed. "Wow, this is so good. What do you guys think?"

"Um, this is great!" Lowell spoke as he swallowed the meat. "It is not that oily I presume."

"Yeah, and it is so yummy!" Cathy squealed as she giggled in happiness.

I giggled too and then glanced at Charles. Charles caught my eye and smiled.

"I loved reading books in my castle's library, when I was in my early teenage hood," He started his story, and we listened. "So I begged my father to make a huge library just for me, and I started to collect books in there like I was opening my own library. Then I accumulated thousands of books plus also hundreds of books that my father bought for me."

"What kind of books?" I asked curiously.

"Well, I loved the wild." Charles replied. "I was like a lion in a cage, living in that fabulous but awful castle. So, I loved reading about the living creatures of the wild. Also, I loved to read the stories of survivals in the unknown world."

"Wow that's cool, so you wanted to get away from the castle and just go on an adventure in the wild like, right now?"

"Yeah, I think so." Charles said putting down the leftover bone. He grabbed some plants and raspberries and dropped them into his mouth. I was still holding the meat in my greasy hands. I took another bite from it and listened to him speaking.

"I wanted to go out. I wanted to see the wild lives of the forest even if they were dangerous for me. It was my dream for me to travel on my own. But my father never allowed me. Actually, he got furious when I talked about the wild in front of him. All I could do is to forget about the wild, and continue my studies and practicing my sword fighting skills."

"Adela," Lowell called me as he finished his lunch. "I have been your friend for like years now, and you live in a castle like Charles. I don't remember you complaining you feel like being locked in the castle."

Charles looked surprised. Cathy made a 'hmm' face. I groaned and thought about it for a while. Have I ever felt so locked-in in the castle? Well, I sometimes felt that I was too shy and scared to go out. But, I have never felt like I desire to go out and enjoy what ordinary people do in their ordinary lives. I was too adjusted to the environment of royal settings and acting like royals. Therefore, I have never been curious about wild lives like Charles.

I finally opened my mouth to speak. "Well…yeah. Actually I have never felt like going out and traveling the wild like Charles did. I read some stories about natures and stuff like that. But they did not pull my interest much."

"Then what are you interested in?" Charles asked.

"She is interested in social studies and history. Adel is really good at it," Cathy answered. "right, Adela?"

"Uh…I guess." I put down the bone and wiped my greasy mouth.

"I always felt that I am different from others and I get my freedom limited compared to the ordinary people. But I accepted what I was given. I was like, this is my fate, and I need to live like this…I can't change it."

There was silence. Cathy and Lowell were nodding and Charles was staring at me. I stared back and he leaned over at me. He stared at me with his glistening eyes. "Do you believe in fate, Adela?"

I was startled by his sudden question. But, I made up my mind quickly and said,

"Yes, I do."

Information

Charles and I had many conversations walking miles of roads and climbing hills until night. It was my first time walking through forests and climbing huge hills, so my legs were pretty numb and they were shaking hard that I collapsed down some times.

Charles said that I needed to exercise more than sitting in the castle. Well, I guess what he said to me was true, but I'd rather memorize a whole dictionary than doing fitness everyday for my whole life.

Anyway, I thought maybe I should record what he says since he said that I needed to keep in mind his sayings. I looked back to my memory and started writing on my notepad that I brought.

<Our ways during the quest>

First- Devina: the country is full of fruits, vegetables and farms especially pumpkin farms (don't know why they mostly grow pumpkins), also great quality of soil

Second- Elsmiere (where Charles was from): the country with flowers

Third- Lanya: Charles says that this country is very tricky and weird, but I have no idea what he meant by that

Fourth- Aragon (Our final destination): this is my Aunt Beth's country, I read many books about this country, and Aragon is a peninsula facing sea, so it holds many trades with other countries

Danger-Charles told me there is a secret clan living between Lanya and Aragon called Vulgary clan. Vulgary clan is the clan that Aunt Beth had to fight over with. It makes me kind of nervous and Charles says he is too

I closed my notepad and sighed heavily. The stars were shining brightly as the sun went down and the moon showed its bright light. The sky turned dark. I was only with Cathy because boys went out to find some more woods for the fire. The fire was dying slowly and the flame started to go out. I glanced at Cathy reading the book that I lent her.

"Hey," I giggled and yelled. "That's 'The Sorrows of Young Werther', the book that I lent you!"

"Yeah, I am almost halfway through the book." Cathy said with her eyes locked on the book.

"How do you like it?"

"Um…I totally love it!" Cathy exclaimed in excitement. "I am reading the part when Albert is back and poor Werther is moaning inside. Wow I mean, this book is pretty old isn't it? But it gives me the real emotion of love and desire."

"Yes, the book is filled with so much emotion. I always cry whenever I read this. Have you ever cried while reading books?"

"Um, I don't really remember. I think I have… it was called 'The War Games', I think. There were many soldiers dying in that book and the part when the young soldier who is 10 years old said that 'War is like a game and it is my life. I play this kind of game to end it quick.' That quote made my tears gather." Cathy's eyes twinkled with a stream of her tear. I smiled at her.

"Hmm, 'The War Games'…I will have a chance to read it someday. I should go to the library to borrow it." I said as I watched her wipe her tears with her sleeves.

"We are back ladies." Charles dropped the woods onto the fire and knelt down. He started to blow the dying fire and Lowell appeared behind him. Lowell also dropped the woods to the fire and settled down next to me. Cathy blushed a little and quickly put her book into her bag.

"Now we got plenty of woods." Lowell smiled with his sweetest dimple.

"Ladies, we know that we are all hungry, so Lowell and I picked some edible flowers and mushrooms from the forest."

"Yippee!" Cathy exclaimed in joy. "Oh my goodness, I was so hungry."

Actually, we were all starving to death. We haven't eaten anything except the little amount of rabbit meat and some plants. We ate too little for lunch and depleted our energy, so we needed food to gain energy again.

But the problem was, the food was too little. Even after we finished everything that Charles brought, we were still hungry.

Charles was looking like he was sorry. "I am so sorry. But don't worry. We will eat so much food when we get to Devina."

"How much is it left to get there?" Cathy asked.

"Well," Charles thought for a minute and answered. "It will take about just a day. I thought it'll take more than 2 days, but I realized that we walk very fast."

"That's good news." Lowell said as he rubbed his stomach with hunger. "I heard that there is a lot of food to eat in Devina because the people living there have enormous farmlands."

"I want to have some muffins," Cathy grumbled. "At the Muffin Divers."

I giggled and stared at the dark black sky. The moon was shining brightly as it laid softly on the clouds. I have never seen the moon so big and bright like this before. Such a peaceful night for such a peaceful dream…

Strange Dream

I could not move my legs. I could not move my arms, not even my finger tips. I was frozen. Heavy thick air covered my breath and I could hardly breathe. I shouted for help as loudly as I could. But there was nothing around me. Closing my eyes, I could feel my hope fading out.

Suddenly, I heard a tingling noise and I opened my eyes. There was Charles, standing far away. I shouted for him as hard as I could, but he did not come for me. He glared at me and yelled back at me.

"Adela, you are not with us, are you? You betrayed us."

What the heck is he talking about? I was confused for a second. I thought about what I did over and over again, but I could not figure out what I did to them.

However, Charles shook his head like there was nothing I could do and slowly moved far away from me. I became impatient and thought over and over about what I did to them.

"No! Charles please don't go!" I shouted as hard as I could. However, my voice was too small for him to hear. He faded away slowly, and I pulled my legs to run to him. Charles started to disappear completely from my eyes and I was anxious and scared to death.

"Please, no...Charles come back to me...I am so sorry about everything...everything..."

"Adela…Adela…are you okay?"

"Wha…what?"

I opened my heavy eyelids. I could see the clear blue sky right in front of me. I could see Cathy and Lowell looking at me nervously.

It was a dream.

"Oh my god," My clothes were wet with my sweat. I could feel my sweat running down my forehead. I was so glad that that horrible dream was over and not real.

"That was the weirdest dream ever." I choked out as they knelt down, staring at me.

Lowell sat next to me and asked. "What did you dream of?"

I smiled at him. "I could not move a tiny bit of my body. I was reaching for you guys, but you were like, 'You betrayed us. We can't take you on quest.'"

"Bad dreams, bad dreams," Cathy laughed. "It doesn't mean anything Adela. Why would you be so scared?"

"Because in that dream, I was in the middle of nowhere. Think about it Cathy. If you don't know the way to your home and your friends are leaving you, how would you feel?"

Cathy thought for a minute. "Well, I would just wander around and start a new life."

"What?" Lowell burst out laughing. "Cathy, are you sure about that?"

"Yeah, why should I be scared? Anyway, this is what I'd do."

I shook my head and smiled at her. "Cathy, you are so brave about everything. That's one of the parts that I like about you."

"Guys," Charles appeared holding a rope. Down the rope, there was a little deer, its neck wrapped with the rope. My mouth could not shut.

"What is that…" I muttered. I looked around at Cathy and Lowell. They were excited to see the deer caught. They may be thinking, wow we are finally going to fill our tummy with such a delicious meal today. But I was different.

When I first saw the sobbing deer in Charles' hands, there was a picture that was drawn in my mind.

It reminded me of my pet deer, named Connie. I was 4 years old when I got her for my birthday. I always played with her in the garden. She was so friendly and a little shy, I remember. I always played with her with a small ball. She was rolling the ball with her nose and I ran after it to catch and threw it high. Then Connie would catch it, bite into the ball and spit it right in front of me. We repeated this during the whole afternoon. But, the happiness did not last long for each of us. One day, Connie accidently broke her leg when she was playing with me and went to the hospital. Her doctor said she is getting too old and she will die soon. I did not hear this news because my mother did not want me to know about death in my early age. At first, my body guard Michael heard the news and he was not allowed to tell me. When Connie died, Michael told me that Connie went back to her mother again. I was so disappointed that I did not come out of my room for hours. I did not even eat my lunch and dinner. My father was worried about me and Brianna kept knocking on my door for hours. At last, they opened my door with the key and found me crying in my bed.

Brianna ran to me and hugged me tightly. She looked worried.

"Oh, miss princess," She wailed and sobbed a little. "I was so worried that you will be so disappointed."

I lifted my head and stared at Brie with my red swollen eyes. I hugged her back and started to cry hard.

"Brianna," I sobbed. "My friend Connie is gone now. I think she totally forgot about me. Or maybe she doesn't like me anymore because I took all of her toys. Or maybe she hates me now because I did not feed her properly."

"No, no princess, don't say that." Brianna stroked my head gently. "It is not because of you. She is gone on a vacation. That's all."

I wiped my tears off and stared at her with my eyes bigger than before. "Oh, really? She is on vacation?"

Brianna smiled softly. "Of course, she wanted to meet her mother and spend some time with her for a while. She will come back tomorrow. I promise."

I smiled and jumped up and down and screamed with joy. My mother and father watched that situation and slowly walked away.

After that event happened, Michael bought a new deer that looked almost the same with Connie and told me that Connie was back. But the new deer didn't know how to play with the ball. It's weird, I thought. But I thought that Connie forgot about the ball when she was meeting her mother. I taught her how to play again and she became just like real

Connie.

"Adela?"

I looked up. I shook my head gently and opened my mouth.

"Sorry, I was in my flashback."

That time I felt my eyes wet. Charles chuckled and sighed. "So, are we going to cook or not?"

My eyes got bigger. "Wait…no!"

Everyone glanced at me. "What's wrong Adela?"

My fists trembled slightly as I stared at Charles to speak. But I couldn't say something properly. I was not sure how I was feeling back then. Was I doing the right thing? I was not sure why and how I was thinking this.

"Uh…I…know…everyone's going to disapprove to this…but…I am kind of desperate."

I closed my eyes and thought about Connie and opened my eyes and looked at the deer. That time, I realized that that deer had similar eyes with Connie; her dark eyes full of purity and nature. I smiled and took the rope from Charles' hand and stared at everyone.

"Guys, we can't eat this. I know this is very stupid and foolish,"

I slipped the rope from my hand and the rope fell to the ground. The nervous deer turned its head to my hand. Then, it stared at my eyes, like it was saying 'thank you' to me.

Everyone stared absentmindedly with their mouth open. I knew they may be thinking, 'Oh my god, she must be out of her mind. She just let go of the rope when we are about to starve to death.'

"A..dela…" Cathy first let out a whisper. As Cathy approached to grab the rope again, the deer ran away swiftly through the grass.

"I am so sorry, guys," I glanced at everyone's face. "It reminded me of my pet deer that passed away when I was young. Back then, it was my first time I experienced death. I couldn't help it."

Lowell nodded. "Well, sometimes you don't want to eat meat when you see how they die," Lowell put his hand on my shoulder. "I understand."

Charles shrugged. "Well, should we go vegetarian from now on then?"

I saw Cathy's face go white. I knew she couldn't stand veggies without meat. I shook my head gently and smiled.

"Of course not, I only don't want deers to be sacrificed in our quest."

That morning we had to eat small amount of edible plants that Charles brought. I chewed boringly and so did my companies.

"Hey," I murmured and everyone looked up. "I am so sorry. I know that deer gets caught rarely, but…"

"Nah, it's all right," Lowell stood up from his seat and smiled brightly.

"Veggies are better for our bodies, and I bet it will help us get healthier."

"Well, meat is much better for our health." Cathy mumbled quietly as she chewed the plant.

"Don't worry. I found out a minute ago that it'll only take less than an hour to get to Devina. I can even prove it."

Cathy looked up at Charles. "How?" she asked curiously.

"Well," Charles pointed with his finger. We followed his look and found out that the soil was much darker brown than the road that we have been walking. It was more like blackish-brown. I touched it and it was so soft. I kept touching it with my hands and so did Lowell.

"The soil is special. It is specially made by Devina people."

"Why is it different? I mean, how?" Lowell asked.

"Well, let me tell you the history of Devina. In ancient times of Devina, there were so many anonymous plants in that country. Those plants covered all parts of Devina so when the first nomads arrived on Devina area, they had to cut off all the plants. But the problem was that they did not know how to get rid of the cut-off plants. So they grinded the plants and just left them in the storage. Many years passed and one day, a prankster came by and unlocked the storage. No one knew that he threw the powder of plants on every farmland. In the morning, people found out their farmlands all spoiled with green powder. Those people had no ways to turn their farmlands back to how they were. So they just left them and left the area. Few months passed and there were other nomads coming into Devina area. When they saw the left-alone farmlands, they were surprised. It was because the seeds grew into such delicious fruits and veggies with no insect bites. They tasted them and they concluded that they were excellent."

"So those nomads figured out that the powder helped the plants grow and those people decided to live here and throw grinded plants onto the ground. So that's why the soil looks different from other soils."

Lowell explained his guess. Charles nodded.

"You're quite right actually. He explained it all. They call their soil, 'Mirari', which means 'miracle' in English."

"That's cool. Wow, how interesting." Cathy murmured. She hated history more than anything. Once in middle school she wrote a short essay of 'why should we not study history'. That blew everyone up! I giggled as I had a flashback of Cathy getting an F for that essay.

"Why are you giggling?" Cathy asked, squinting her eyes.

I shook my head. "Nah, I just had a flashback."

"Now we took some rest and learned about history of Devina, let's go!"

Charles led us in front. We followed him behind and started chatting again.

"I am so hungry," Cathy moaned. "just like I haven't eaten for a month."

I looked at my stomach. It was caved in and as I ran my finger down my chest, I realized I could feel my ribs. I needed to eat something. I was desperate for the juicy beef steak cooked with garlic sauce that our chef invented. I was desperate for the sweetest and creamy chocolate mousse that I enjoyed to eat when I was back at home.

Home, sweet home. I really missed Brianna. She would laugh if she knew I miss her even if it has only been a day leaving Anastelon.

Charles smirked and tapped Cathy's shoulder.

"Don't worry. We only have to walk for a little and after that, we can go inside any house and eat as much food as you want. Devina people love to share with people, and in that country, there is no king or queen. The most surprising thing is that they don't have stores. When their food lack, they ask for food from their neighbors. They hold a party once a month, just like Thanksgiving Day. I'd been to that party once, and it was so marvelous."

Cathy's stomach rumbled to death. "All right, all right, please don't make me die of hunger."

"Of course not." Charles smiled.

Devina

We arrived in Devina, finally. I could see the full grown tomatoes hanging onto the sprig. I wanted to pluck it off and bite into its sweetness. But, I endured.

"Let's go to that house over there." Charles pointed and I could see a white house with red roof. It was near to our standing spot, thank god.

We walked to that house and I knocked on the door. I could hear the chair dragging slowly. "Who is it?" I could barely hear an old man's unclear voice. Charles shouted out loud on the door.

"Grandpa Louis, it's me, Charles from Elsmiere."

There was a short hesitation. I heard a few small footsteps. The door was opened and there stood a little old man with small glasses and a cane. He was a hunchback, and he looked like as if he was going to fall in a moment.

"Oh, Charles, my dear. I am so glad you visit me again. Last time you came alone, but this time, you brought your wonderful friends along! Come and sit around the table."

Grandpa Louis ushered us to the dining room and shouted at the kitchen.

"Hey Sarah darling, there are some special guests from other countries. Bring us some delicious food to eat. Please hurry though."

"All right." A high tone voice replied back at grandpa Louis.

We sat around the table and Charles started to introduce all of us. He told Grandpa Louis that we were going on a quest for me to receive the throne.

"Well," Grandpa Louis nodded and smiled in comfort. "Let me introduce myself. My name is Louis Jamie McCarthy. My wife is Sarah. You can call me Grandpa Louie by the way. It sounds cuter that Louis." Grandpa Louis chuckled and so did everyone. Sarah appeared from the kitchen. She had red hair with freckles around her nose. She looked so young and I couldn't not believe that she was 67 years old.

"Hello," She smiled and glanced at each one of us. She stared at me for a long time and opened her mouth.

"Oh my god, are you the princess of..."

"Yes, I am the princess of Anastelon. It's such a pleasure to meet you Sarah." I grinned at her.

"Oh, Adela my dear," She suddenly ran into me and hugged tightly.

"You've grown up so much. Wow, I first didn't recognize you because the first time I saw you, was on your birthday when you were a year old! Oh my god, oh my god..."

She hugged me for 2 or 3 minutes and let me go. She wiped her tears and stared at my face again.

"You are so gorgeous Miss Adela Monette. You are the most beautiful girl I've ever seen."

She's got to be kidding. That time, I looked like a girl from a trash can.

I sniffed to see how I smelled. Ew, I don't remember eating rotten eggs during the quest.

"Oh, the soup is ready. I will go get it quickly."

Sarah ran to the kitchen and carried bowls of tomato soup to the table. Lastly, she carried 3 dishes of salad to the middle of the table.

"There you go. Enjoy the soup. It is really good. Oh, and try some salad for appetizer."

Sarah disappeared into the kitchen. Grandpa Louie glanced at us and smiled. "Well, you haven't eaten a proper meal. Please enjoy the meal."

"Thank you very much." Charles said and started to eat the soup.

I did not have time to hesitate. I picked the spoon and gulped the tomato soup down my throat. Mmmm…the tomatoes were so sweet and a little bit sour. I loved it. I did not have time to think anything.

I finished the soup in just one minute. Then, I grabbed the fork and shoved the salad into my mouth. Mmmm…this is just great. It just feels like I am home.

While I was eating, I glanced at Cathy, who was eating in the fastest speed between four of us. But, she stopped eating and waited for the meat to come.

About 15 minutes later, Sarah called out. "Goose is ready to be served."

She brought a huge goose meat cooked with garlic sauce and all kinds of veggies. The goose looked so delicious that I wanted to dive into it. As she put the goose in the middle of the table, we dove our forks and knives and started to cut the meat.

I shoved a piece into my mouth. Oh my god, it was just so delicious. I have eaten geese for many times before back in my castle, but they weren't as good as this one.

I cut another piece of meat and chewed. I could feel the soft and juicy meat running down my throat. It was the most delicious meal ever.

"That was so delicious." Cathy said rubbing her stomach.

We sat down in the living room, chatting about Devina's culture.

"People in Devina eat tomato soup for every meal," Grandpa Louie said. "It is the oldest tradition in here."

I jumped up. "So, you have eaten this tomato soup for every meal? Are you sure you never have forgotten to eat the soup?"

"No, not even once," Grandpa Louie chuckled. "Sarah is such a diligent woman she never forgets anything."

"You're so lucky to eat this delicious soup for every meal." Lowell commented.

Cathy shrugged in confusion. "Well, in my opinion if that was me, I will be sick of eating that soup. What do you think Grandpa Louie?"

Grandpa Louie thought and smiled in his gentle dimples. "Well, it is good for ingesting proper amount of nutrition for each day. Actually, we have lots of tomatoes growing in Devina, so we should get rid of them by eating them for every meal."

Everyone laughed and I listened to them talking as I massaged my swollen legs. They were sore from walking for so long.

Charles stared at me massaging and said, "Adela, you should go to sleep. You look so tired right now."

Lowell yawned and stood up from his seat. "Aww, I need to take a shower. Can I use the bathroom Grandpa Louie?"

Grandpa Louie grinned. "Of course you can. The bathroom is near your rooms. First Sarah, please lead them to their bedrooms. They look so tired from their long travel."

Sarah smiled and ushered us to a hall. She lit the lights and the hall got bright. Then, I could see dozens of guestrooms down the hall. My mouth made a shape like an 'o' because when I saw Grandpa Louie's house outside, it didn't look big enough to be holding so many guestrooms inside.

"Wow, Sarah, is this house used for motel or something?" I asked as I looked around.

Sarah laughed. She walked fast down the hall and we followed after her. Then she stopped and turned right. There, we could see a wide door. Sarah took out the keys and unlocked it.

"Well, there are many visitors and wanderers visiting our country. My husband and I decided to take care of them when they visit out country."

"That's nice." Cathy lifted her thumb up and grinned.

Sarah opened the door. The smell of pine tree tickled my nostrils. Sarah turned on the lights and we could see a wide room.

There were two beds, a wooden table, a fireplace, a wide window and a closet. It was quite nice. I could say that it was much better than a hotel suite.

"This room is for girls," Sarah said and put some woods into the fireplace. She lit the fire with her lighter and stood up.

"I am pretty sure your clothes may have been dirty from the travel. If you have dirty clothes, put them in that basket." She pointed at the corner of the room. I could see a small basket next to one of the beds.

Cathy and I smiled at Sarah. "Thank you so much Sarah, for everything."

Sarah was about to go out of the room. But she suddenly turned back at us and asked. "Oh, I almost forgot. When will you leave our country?"

"Well, we will leave in two days." Charles answered.

"Oh my god, then you are going to attend the party, right? We have this huge Thanksgiving party once a month. Please say that you will."

Catherine jumped up and down. "Oh, really? Wow, of course we will. I am definitely going to go. Aren't we guys?"

Charles nodded. "Sure, why not?"

"Oh, and I forgot. Devina people will all speak English when there are visitors, so you don't have to worry about communication." Sarah said.

I jumped up and down excitedly with Cathy. Then I realized I did not have the clothes to wear for the party. Cathy seemed to realize that too. We stopped laughing crazily.

"But, we do not have any clothes for the party," She mumbled. "We can't have fun at the party if we are looking like garbage."

We thought for a moment. Suddenly, Sarah clicked her fingers and looked up.

"Don't worry guys. I have this friend who collects hundreds of party clothes. I borrowed from her once, and it was quite nice. Tomorrow morning, after breakfast, I will take you to her. Problem solved?"

We smiled simultaneously. "Problem solved." I answered.

Party

"Come on! Girls. We should hurry. I need to get you the prettiest clothes from her."

We hurried up and put on our clothes. I tied up my long hair in one ponytail and Cathy left her super-curly hair loose. She always had kept her hair up, but when she let her hair down, she looked much more feminine.

We walked down the road and I walked between Charles and Cathy. Lowell seemed as he wanted to talk to me. I smiled and walked over to him.

"How was your room?" I asked.

He shrugged. "Well, it was not bad. Actually, I thought it was a little better than hotel rooms."

"Wow, that's what I thought last night. Was your room just like ours?"

"Well, yeah, it was. It was quite similar."

Lowell seemed a little disappointed and gloomy. I glanced at his face and asked.

"Are you okay? You seem upset. Is there something wrong?"

Lowell looked up and looked at me. He smiled in his usual smile.

"Nah, I'm fine."

It was kind of weird. He seemed down since the first day of the quest. Is he regretting that he followed me to the quest? Maybe he still wants to study in high school instead of following me in this quest. Actually, I fully understand his feelings. He studied so much to go to the most prestigious university in Anastelon. He was planning to reach his goal. He always wanted to be a professor. I've got to help him. When I get back to my country, I will definitely ask my father to make Lowell to be the most famous professor in our country.

"We are here."

I looked up and so did everyone. There was a small house on a small hill. We climbed up and Sarah knocked the door.

There was a small footstep inside and the door opened slightly.

"Who is it?" A young woman stepped out from the house. She looked like she was in the early thirties. She had scarlet hair with green eyes and thick lips. She glanced at Sarah and then every one of us. Finally, she smiled and let us in.

Sarah opened her mouth. "I brought the visitors from other country. They are royal, so please bring the most high-quality clothes for them to wear for tonight's party."

"Sure," A young woman answered. Then she disappeared into a huge closet. Minutes later, the young woman appeared out of the closet, holding dozens of colorful short dresses and dozens of suits.

"Oh, and I forgot to introduce myself. My name is Scarlett. You see, my hair is really, really red, so I was named Scarlett. It's easy peasy."

"So, Scarlett, please hold up the clothes for us to see."

"Sure."

Scarlett first held up a purple dress. Cathy and I took a glance. The dress was filled with laces and beads, but it was not my kind of dress.

We both shrugged. Then, Scarlett held up another dress, which was yellow. It was a simple dress and it was very pretty. Cathy jumped up and held the dress. She held it in front of her body to see if it fits her.

"Oh my god, it is totally my style. How do I look?"

She stood in front of a big mirror and smiled big as she can as if she was a model. I clapped my hands.

"Wow, Cathy, you look so gorgeous. I love that dress. I think it is perfect for getting attention in the party. You look like a shining star, Cathy."

Cathy grinned. "I will wear this one for the party."

Scarlett held up another dress. It was light pink with little laces on lower parts. It was almost as pretty as the ones that I wear in the castle. I grabbed that pink dress and held it up in front of me.

"Oh my god, this one is so pretty. How do I look, Cathy?"

Cathy glanced at me and smiled. "Wow, you are the queen."

I blushed and turned around for Sarah to see. The boys were out of the room for surprise.

Sarah clapped her hands. "Why, you two look just like princesses! Well, Adela, I think you really fit the image of a princess, and Cathy, you shine, like a star."

"You chose your dresses, then go to the dressing room. There will be make-up materials that you can put on. Those things you can do by yourselves, right?"

"Sure, thanks Scarlett." I said and we both left the room, holding our dresses. We wore our dress and put the make-ups on. It was a little hard for me, because I hardly put make-ups when I was back in the castle. My mother did not let me put make-ups frequently because they may hurt my skin. But it was a relief that we both knew how to put on make-ups.

"I wouldn't make myself look like Lindsay, will I?" I joked and put on the mascara on both eyes. Cathy giggled.

"No, that would be terrible. Don't worry. You look so beautiful, Adela, even without make-ups. I am actually afraid that you will look so pretty that everyone will think that I am so ugly."

"What? You are the cutest, and the prettiest friend I have ever seen, Cathy. Don't you be so pessimistic about yourself!"

"But, why wouldn't Lowell seem like he has a crush on me? He seems to like you more than me. He is never interested in me."

"Oh, please Cathy, don't think like that. I am helping you. I am trying to fix his thoughts to make him have good impressions on you."

"Ugh, it has been years. Why wouldn't he even take a move?"

"He is shy and dense. That's why. I have known him since we were so young. I know everything about him. I know how to manage him."

We had a long conversation about Lowell. I promised her again that I will make him like Cathy. I always try to make Lowell like Cathy. For example, first I made Cathy do the group work with Lowell. Then, they seemed to be closer. I also made Cathy to give chocolates and a letter saying: 'I wish we could be much closer.' on Valentine's Day. I was trying to drop a little hint to Lowell that Cathy is crushing on him, but he was so dense. Also, Cathy and I tried to spread a rumor that Cathy likes Lowell, but when Lowell heard that rumor, he did not believe it. He said, "Of course not, Cathy thinks of me as her best friend. She wouldn't break our friendship like that." And he laughed off. For heaven's sake, he was the densest person on planet!

When we finished putting our make-ups, we waited for the boys. Time flew so fast and when I looked out the window, it was dark.

"Jeez, we used so much time on this job." Cathy murmured.

Sarah appeared in front of the door. "Girls, please wait outside the party place. I think this may take a little bit longer."

So we went outside and the party was getting almost ready. There were stands and tables with lots of foods on them. There were also games stalls and a show stage. It was a large party and everyone looked so excited and hyper. I looked around and I saw the placards and posters coming up saying, 'Fresh lemon juice from the Alfred's', 'Sweet yams cooked by Mama Jacquie', 'Crispy vegetarian Toasts from Kingsley's' and so on. There were hundreds of food stalls with many kinds of foods, which especially contained veggies. My mouth watered as I waited for the dark to arrive.

The street seemed to be fulfilled with so many people. I was so surprised that it was so different from when it was morning because I could hardly see a person walking in the morning. But now, there were hundreds of people preparing for this huge celebration.

Then, I suddenly realized people moving toward the stage. It seemed everyone was moving toward the stage. Cathy shrugged and followed after the people and so did I.

"Why are they moving to the stage?" I asked.

"Maybe there will be a show or concert or...something. I don't know, let's just follow them and see what they are up to." Cathy mumbled and pulled my arm.

We stood in the middle of the crowd and stood on our toes to see.

The red curtain shuffled open. There stood an old man in a suit with a long grey mustache. He cleared his throat and started to talk on the microphone.

"Ahem, hello everyone, welcome to our Thanksgiving festival,"

People started to clap for a long, long period. Then it ended slowly.

"Today's party is very special. First, let me introduce these great fruits and veggies that Jamie grew for a month. He grew tomatoes, apples and oranges."

Huge chunks of fruits stood on the table. Everyone hollered and screamed, "Best Devruits! Best Deveggies!"

"What do 'Devruits' and 'Deveggies' mean?" Cathy asked.

"'Devruits' is a combination of Devina and fruits, and 'Deveggies' is a combination of Devina and veggies," I answered. "Haven't you heard of them? They are pretty famous."

Cathy shrugged. "Well, I hate veggies. I have never been interested in veggies and fruits. I think that's why I have never heard of them."

After we chat, the old man on stage seemed to finish talking about how they grew veggies and fruits in such special ways.

"Secondly, we have new visitors, who visited our country. Please come on upstage."

There was a silence. I quickly pulled Cathy and brought myself and Cathy upstage. We looked down and saw lots of Devina people glancing at us. I just felt like the moment when I was about to do a speech in front of the Royals back in our castle.

"What about Lowell and Charles? They are visitors too!" Cathy squeaked and turned around to search for them.

"We are here, for heaven's sake!" I heard a voice from the other side of the stage. There were Charles and Lowell running toward us, in their nice formal suits. Charles looked just gorgeous and I was so glad that they came. I wanted to hug Charles...wait, what was I thinking?

Oh my god, am I falling for this gorgeous looking prince who is going to lead me throughout the whole quest?

"Oh my god, you are here!" Cathy jumped up and down in excitement.

"Of course, I am glad we are on time." Lowell grinned and glanced at me up and down with his mouth shaped like an 'o'.

"Oh, Adela," He mumbled. "You look just beautiful."

I giggled and stood between Cathy and Charles. We all faced down the Devina people who were looking back at us.

"Please say a word each, visitors." The old man said on the microphone.

Charles came on front on the microphone and spoke clearly.

"Hello, sweet Devina, I am so happy to attend this wonderful festival with my fellows and our lovely princess, Adela. Please bless Adela for the safe trip, everyone, and I hope you guys to have a good time. Thank you very much." Charles finished and I had to up front and talk. I was quite nervous and I did not know what to say. I hesitated for a moment and opened my mouth.

"Um, thank you for inviting us to this exciting party. Right now, I am so excited for the festival and I hope we all have a good time. Thank you again and I hope you guys have good harvest for this month as well. Thanks." I finished and there was a long clapping from the crowd. Then, it was Cathy's turn to speak. Cathy went up and she made everyone laugh as always. Her speech was pretty funny to listen. After that, it was Lowell's turn. Lowell was a little shy and the old man helped him out to find a topic. He finished his speech neatly and everyone clapped again.

"Now, it's time for our festival, to begin!" The old man shouted so loud on the microphone. Everyone screamed, "Best Devruits! Best Deveggies!" and went to the festival place. We came down the stage and sighed in relief. "Now the festival starts," Lowell said. "I was so nervous on stage and I did not know what to say."

I laughed and pat his back gently. "Nah, don't worry Lowell. You did just fine. Your speech was so neat and cute."

"Yeah, you were the best of four of us," Cathy exaggerated and lifted her thumb up. "I loved your speech Lowell, great job!"

Lowell seemed to be rangy. Oh Cathy, you just exaggerated so much that could have made Lowell lose his word. My thoughts were stuck in my mouth and I couldn't let it out.

"We shouldn't worry about the speeches, they are gone anyway." Charles shouted. "Let's go guys!"

Ugh, there were so many kinds of foods to eat, but my stomach couldn't hold more. Until now, I ate a vegetarian sandwich, some roast meat from a small goose, caesar salad, tomato soup(of course), chocolate cookies, lollies, two pieces of pumpkin pie, and a rice pudding for dessert. Wow, I have never eaten so much food like that before. In my castle, I couldn't eat food much as I wanted because Brianna told me that it is important to keep myself on diet all the time. But I didn't care then. It was such a tiring day and I should provide myself some protein since I am on my Quest.

I saw Cathy eat A LOT. I was worried if she could really become a pig. Gosh, even if I stopped eating, she kept on eating and eating until the festival ended. I bet she ate all kinds of food in the party. She kept on saying, "I have never been so happy in my life." every minute.

The party was going to end soon and I could see it was getting much darker. For last, I grabbed a cup of red wine from a stall and took a sip.

"Taste it," A young man said to me. "My papa and I grew the grapes and made the wine by ourselves. It would taste just great, I can guarantee."

I smiled at him. "I see. It is the best wine I have ever tasted. Thanks so much."

The young man grinned with his freckled cheeks and held out his hand.

"My name's Jeffrey Thomson." He said. I held my hand out and shook his hand.

"Mine's Adela Monette. It's very nice to see you Jeffrey."

"Call me Jeff."

"Well, Jeff," I said and took another sip from the cup. "I am really surprised that you are able to make such great wine like this."

Jeff blushed a little. "Nah, it is my papa doing all the work. He says I am just his helper."

"But, it's still great that you know how the wine gets made. I want to learn how to." I said.

Jeff's face got bright red. "I am not an expertise."

"Here it comes!" Suddenly, there was a loud bang in the sky. The firework show had started!

The sky roared with colorful fireworks. Jeff and I stared at the sky and watched all the explosions going on for a while.

After it ended, Jeff and I both looked at each other and smiled.

"Wow, that was hot, wasn't it?" I asked. Jeff nodded.

"Yeah, I bet that they put on their best fireworks because you guys are here. Last time, the firework only lasted for a minute when we did not have any guests."

"Hey, where have you been?" I turned around and saw Lowell running to me.

"That's what I want to ask to you, Lowell. Where have you been?"

Lowell panted for a while and answered. "I was with Cathy. She keeps on eating by the way. Has she ever been like this before?"

I laughed. "I know eh? She keeps on eating and eating. Maybe she will end up being a pig or something, or maybe she would die as a pig haha!"

"Wait a minute, what are you saying, Miss Adela Monette?"

Uh oh, Cathy was here, and she had heard everything we said about her. I looked at her furious face, that was about to explode.

"Cathy..." I hesitated and tried to think of an excuse, but I couldn't think of any. What should I do?

"Adela, I thought you would always understand how I act and think, just like best friends. But what did you just say? Did you just say that I will end up as a pig? Holy moly, thanks a lot for worrying about me like that Adel. You are the kindest friend I have ever had."

"But Cathy...we were trying to joke, really. We don't mean like that. It's a party Cathy, we were trying to..."

"...Have fun?" Cathy yelled right at my face. Her face got redder. "Is this really fun to you? Great, if making someone watch getting fatter and fatter, laugh it all off. Come on."

"Cathy, we were not making fun of you." Lowell insisted with his serious face. I could see it was getting louder since there was a gambling card games on right next to where we were standing. Lowell grabbed

Cathy's hand and pulled her to the back of the stadium. I saw Cathy's face turn red, as Lowell grabbed her hand so suddenly, but she tried to keep her face angry. Then they disappeared. I looked at Jeff. Jeff noticed my look and shrugged.

"Don't worry. I will wait right here. I totally understand you. Please go."

I smiled at him and ran to where Lowell and Cathy went. I looked around and finally found Lowell and Cathy sitting next to each other on a wooden plank. Cathy was crying with her face still red, and Lowell was patting her back and talking to her. I slowly walked toward them and sat next to Cathy.

"Cathy," I whispered. "I am so, deadly, sorry."

Cathy held her head up. I could fully see her red face smothered with tears. "Sorry for what? For me being like a pig?"

"No," I shouted. "I am so, so sorry for being so stupid and selfish. I shouldn't have said anything bad like that. I was so hyper that I forgot the manners that we had to keep between friends. I am so sorry, Cathy. I promise it will never happen again, I swear."

Cathy wiped off her tears. "Are you sure about that?"

I smiled. "Of course I am sure. Come on, everyone's waiting."

I jumped up and pulled Cathy. She and Lowell stood up and we walked back to where we were from. I could see Lowell was still holding her hand tightly. I am pretty sure Cathy was screaming on the inside.

Jeff was still there, waiting for us. "There you are!" Jeff said as we stood in front of him. "Did it work out well?"

I smiled and looked at both Cathy and Lowell. "Well, pretty much. But I still feel so sorry and guilty."

I was so sure today had worked out so well, even when I was caught making fun of Cathy. I caught every movement that Lowell did to Cathy and he took care of her that night just as if she was her girlfriend! Wow, I had never seen Lowell being so gentle like that. Because of that, Cathy's feelings got better and better, and started to giggle when we were chatting. It was when we were sitting next to the fire, which we made for campfire near Jeff's house. We all got closer to Jeff since he was so nice and funny. He usually talked about those weird and strange things that he finds when he is helping his father. It may be boring to some people, but his eloquence was interesting to listen. I got a lot closer to Jeff, and it was strange how I could easily understand the differences between us.

But sadly, it was almost midnight, so we had to sleep for tomorrow.

"Good night!" I said and waved my hand to Jeff.

Devina's beauty

I woke up during the night. It was another nightmare. I could feel the chills running down my back. I wiped off my sweat and tried to sleep, but I couldn't. I tried closing my eyes, but I couldn't get into sleep. So, I just lay down there and looked up the ceiling. The ceiling looked a little old and dark. Actually, everything was dark around me. All I could hear was a quiet snore from Cathy's bed.

Suddenly, there was a loud rustling sound from outside. Oh my god, could it be a ghost? I thought. The rustling got bigger and bigger, and I could see the tree was shaking. Maybe I am still in my nightmare, I thought. Wake up, wake up! I closed my eyes and tried to wake myself up.

Then, there were knocks on the window. I didn't dare to open my eyes. I could feel the goosebumps lying on every part of my body. Who's that? I wondered, but still did not dare to see who it was.

Two knocks. I started to freak out, but couldn't scream because I may wake everyone up. But, suddenly, I heard a voice that was familiar.

"Hey, Adela." It was calling me from outside.

I finally opened my eyes and saw Jeff standing outside the window.

I made my mouth shape like an 'o' and quietly ran to the window.

"Oh my god," I whispered. "You totally scared me to death!"

Jeff laughed in his cute smile. "Come out Adel, I want to take you somewhere."

"What? You mean right now?" I asked.

"Yup," He said. "You don't have to get changed. Come out in your pajamas."

I quickly wore my hood jacket and hurriedly but carefully opened the window. I checked on Cathy every second and Jeff helped me out of the room. It took a long time, but it was fun since it was with Jeff.

Finally, I was out. It was freezing outside. The icy air gave me more chills.

"I didn't know you would feel cold," He said. "In Devina, it is warm at days and cold at nights. Here, take this."

He wrapped my body with his warm jacket. After I wore it, I felt much better. The jacket smelled like pine trees.

"Thanks," I said. "That feels better."

We kept on walking and walking without any word. So, I asked him, "You told me that you want to take me somewhere."

Jeff smiled. "Yep, and we are going in the right way. Come on, it is not that far from here."

Jeff started to run. I started funning too and followed his back. When we stopped running, we were on a huge cliff.

I breathed hard and looked at Jeff. "So, this is the place?" I asked.

"Yes, it is."

"What are we doing here?"

Jeff turned around and faced the sky. I followed his stare and saw the scarlet light streaming up to the sky. It was the sun, rising with its beautiful, round shape.

"Oh my god," I squealed. "We are here to watch the sunrise?"

Jeff turned to me and nodded. I smiled at him. It was my first time seeing the sun so big and bright like this, and it was also my first time, watching the sun rise right in front of me.

"It's so beautiful." I murmured as the blazing sun shone its light upon us.

Jeff stood next to me and whispered. "Not as beautiful as you, Miss Adela."

Jeff was so sweet and kind. I gave him a hug and after we saw the full sun, he walked with me to the window where I came out from.

We stopped when we arrived and I turned back to Jeff.

"Thank you, Jeff. That was so beautiful." I said.

Jeff chuckled. "Not at all. It was my pleasure to take you there. Maybe I can take you somewhere more wonderful tomorrow. If you wish, I could take you sightseeing tour in Devina."

Then I realized, that I did not tell Jeff that I was leaving today. I opened my mouth to speak. "Hey, Jeff, I need to tell you..."

But my word was cut when Jeff's father was calling him from far away. Jeff's eyes got bigger and stared at my eyes.

"I gotta go, Adela. See ya." He turned around and was about to run, but he stopped. Then he turned back to me and sweetly kissed my hand. I could feel my heart beating so loudly in my chest, and my cheeks felt so hot. I could not say anything to him. Before I said anything, he just ran to his father. I stared his back when he ran, with my heart pounding like it will explode. When Jeff disappeared from my sight, I opened the window and went inside.

I could see Cathy was still sleeping and snoring. I quickly and carefully reached my hand to take off my jacket, but then I noticed I was still wearing his jacket. Uh oh, I completely forgot about this. Maybe, I will give this to him before I leave Devina, which is this morning.

"What are you doing over there Adela?" Suddenly, I heard Cathy's voice from behind me. I was so surprised. So, I turned around to her and smiled.

"I couldn't sleep," I told her. "I was wondering if I could take a walk on the roads or something."

Cathy's eyes got bigger. "Are you crazy? It's only 6:45 AM in the morning. You can take more than a walk on our way to Elsmiere."

"Oh, right," I said and took off my jacket. "I forgot."

I walked toward my bed and lay down as Cathy covered his head with the blanket and snored in few seconds. My eyelids were getting heavier and when I closed my eyes, I fell asleep right away.

"Pack up girls!" Charles shouted at Cathy and me as we ran down the hall to our room. We gathered our clothes and put them in our bags. I filled my water bottle with the water from the tap. Then I put the dress that Scarlett gave us for souvenir.

"Take 'em all," Scarlett told us, when we went to her house with the dresses we borrowed. "I have lots of other dresses. I want you to keep them and think of Devina whenever you see those beautiful dresses."

I was once glad, but felt a little upset for my bag getting so full of lacy dress. When I stuffed my dress into my tiny bag, my bag was about to explode.

Cathy and I finished packing up and got out of our room. I was carrying my small backpack and holding Jeff's jacket on my left arm.

Lowell saw the jacket and asked.

"Isn't that a man's clothes?"

I was startled. "Uh…well…Lowell…yesterday, Jeff lent me his clothes because I felt cold. But I forgot to give this back to him."

Lowell didn't say a word. He hardly says anything these days. Gosh, isn't he still getting over with this school marks? If he is, he is so adhesive. It kind of makes me upset now seeing him acting so weirdly these days. But the good thing is that he is much closer to Cathy.

"Come on guys, hurry up." Charles yelled.

"Wait, Charles," I ran to him and said. "I need to say goodbye to Jeff, Please wait for a minute, please."

When I begged, he nodded. "Go on, but please hurry. We should leave quickly to arrive at the exact time."

"Okay."

I ran to where Jeff lived. I ran and ran as fast as I could and when I finally arrived in front of his house, I could see Jeff was watering the flowers in the garden.

"Hey, Adela," He squealed in happiness when he saw me running toward him. "You are here so early. Are you here to ask me for sightseeing?"

I kept breathing so hard and fast since I ran so fast. When my breath got comfortable, I was able to speak.

"Jeff," I said and stood closer to him. "Here's your jacket."

"Oh, thanks. But I wanted you to have it. It looks better on you."

"No," I whispered and I could feel the tears gathering in my eyes. Then, there was a big lump in my throat.

"I can't keep it. It's yours, Jeff."

I handed the jacket over to him. He received it from me.

"Thanks. Adela." He smiled at me so sweetly.

"Jeff," I whispered with a tear dropping down my face. "I am leaving right now."

Jeff's smile was washed away. He didn't say anything. He just murmured, "What...?"

"Jeff, I am leaving!" I croaked and cried. It was so strange for me because it only had been two days seeing Jeff and I was crying because I am leaving him. But that time, he felt so special to me.

I wanted Jeff to say a word, but he couldn't. He just stood there, with no expressions on his face. I waited for him to get over with it, but the time was flowing, so I had to leave.

"I've got to go, Jeffrey. I will see you someday, after the quest is finished."

I walked away from him. It was the end. THE END.

Wait, no! It was not the end!

I felt a strong grip on my right hand and I turned around and saw Jeff right in front of me, standing so close.

"Adela," He finally said to me. "I need to tell you something."

My heart was beating and I could almost feel Jeff's heart beat fast.

"Adela," He called me again. "I love you."

I smiled. "I love you too, Jeff. You had been so nice to me for two days."

"Then would you please be my girlfriend?"

What did he just say? My mind went blank. Maybe I heard it wrong. Maybe he was gone out of his mind. I must be dreaming.

I didn't move an inch. I tried to say a word, but couldn't. Finally, I could let my croaking voice out of my mouth.

"Wh...What did you just say to me Jeffrey?"

Jeff sighed with his face red, but determined.

"I said," Jeff blurt it out. "Would you be my girlfriend Adela?"

I felt my heart stop. No, I didn't want this. I never have wanted...oh my god. What should I do? I never have thought him like that.

"Jeffrey, I..." My voice croaked from crying hard. "I am so sorry. I never have thought you like that...I never thought you'd love me so much. I mean, I really love you, like I love Lowell and Cathy, but I don't love you like a crush, Jeff. I am so sorry."

Jeff's face was hardened. His grin and his cute smile disappeared so suddenly. I felt like I have done something so wrong. But a few seconds later, he made up his smile back on his face.

"It's okay, Adela. I fell in love in the first sight when I saw you drinking our wine. You were just so beautiful. It was my first time feeling so passionate. I kept looking at you every minute and every second. Yesterday night, I couldn't sleep because I couldn't stop thinking about your brunette silky hair, your gorgeous smile, and your sweet voice. I wanted to go sightseeing with you and get along together. But, well, it doesn't seem it will come real. It's okay Adela. You shouldn't be sorry."

He finished his last word, and kissed my hand again, just like he did last night. He was just too sweet to me. I smiled and wiped off my tears. He lowered his head and let his tears flow down his cheeks. Now I could totally understand how he felt that time. He was so desperate. He didn't want to spoil the time with me, but I couldn't do anything about it, and I didn't love him as much as he did love me.

I lifted his head up with my both hands and stared at his red eyes. His dazzling eyes stared right at me, still so desperate. I couldn't help it. My lips automatically touched his soft cheek.

"Good bye, Jeff." I whispered for the last time, and then I walked away from him.

I have never loved someone so desperately in my life, like Jeff, but I knew how Jeff felt, just by staring at his eyes. That time, I have never felt so sorry before. It gave me heartache for a long time.

There are many people who are in love together, or someone crushing on somebody, but in my memory, I have never loved anyone. My mother once told me that I loved a handsome boy when I was in the kindergarten. But I couldn't remember who he was and what happened then.

To me, love means 'feeling the heart ache when you see someone not interested in you' or 'feeling so desperate and passionate', just like Jeff. I have seen many people in love in our school. Those tied-together-couples, Kayleigh and Cameron, Lindsay and Tony, Olivia and Andy are just so in love with each other in our St. Luke's High school. Of course, I sometimes get confessions from many guys in school, but I told all of them that I wanted to stay as friends. I didn't know why I didn't feel true love beyond those hundreds of guys who confessed to me. Maybe it was because my mother always told me to stay conservative, because I am the princess and I should always be careful.

When I went back to where Charles and my friends were, they were waiting impatiently. But I guessed they couldn't say anything because the quest is on because of me. Before we left the town, many people wanted us to give a lot of their harvested foods, but since we had a long way to travel, we couldn't carry anything heavy. So, Sarah and Grandpa Louie packed us just a small amount of foods which included tomato soup, veggies, some roasted meat and fruits for us to eat on our way. We had to pack the maximum food we can hold because Charles told us that it would take a long time to arrive at Elsmiere. When we were all ready to set, we all waved at the people who were there to send us off.

"Thank you so much people of Devina. We will miss you a lot!" Charles yelled. Everyone cried and waved goodbye. As I stared at their sad faces, they reminded me more of Jeff's red face when he confessed to me. My heart ached more and more as we walked away from them. I wanted to see Jeff for one more time. Maybe Jeff is still crying, or maybe he is trying to get over with it.

I miss you already Jeffrey. But I can't do anything about it. I am still sorry.

"Are you all right, Miss Monette?" Charles asked as he looked at my gloomy and worried face.

I tried to make a smile. "Yeah, I am okay. Thanks for asking."

"You shouldn't be that sad, Adela." Charles shook his head looking worried at me. "You will be leaving so many friends that you make on the way to Aragon, but you are crying too much from the start. How will you enjoy the trip if you are going to miss so many friends like that?"

Charles leaned over me and wiped my wet face. His eyes twinkled in the sunlight. Then I realized that Charles' eyes are very similar to Jeff's eyes. I stared at his dazzling eyes and smiled.

"Sorry. I will try to get over with it, Charles. You don't have to worry about me."

Charles sighed in relief. "That's good. I am sure you will get better when you keep walking. Come on, we are late, guys. Oh, by the way, I didn't tell you that I need to teach you the skills in Elsmiere, did I?"

"What skills?" I asked curiously.

"I am supposed to teach you how to transform into animals and how to fight the Vulgary clan. It is part of our quest and it is a rule for me to teach you. It's because we all need to get rid of the enemies for the peace between the five countries that we are travelling on the quest. I will tell you exactly what you need to do when we arrive at Elsmiere."

"How long would it take to Elsmiere?" Cathy asked.

"Well, in my calculation, it will take…about 4 days. But it still depends on how fast we walk." Ugh, I am sick of walking. Maybe I should have stayed with Jeff in Devina and lie to my father that I finished the quest. It's too bad that it is too late now…All I am facing is all those hundreds of vital enemies who are waiting to kill all of us. Wow, thinking of making peace, it gave me a lot of pressure.

"It gives me a lot of pressure," I said. "Please tell me you had exaggerated the story."

"No, I never tell lies. All I say is the truth, Adela. You will be training with me right after you arrive at Elsmiere."

"But that is too much for me. I mean what if I fail the quest and die in the fight with the enemies? Didn't my father consider that part?"

Charles face hardened. "Don't think of it in such pessimistic way,

Adela. Don't you know the expression, 'we have to stop saying it before it becomes a self fulfilling prophesy'? It means what you say will someday become real. Be careful of what you say. You won't ever die."

"Oh, I get it. You are thinking so optimistic because this task is not on you. Aha! Thanks for giving me much more pressure. I really appreciate it."

"No, I meant even if you die, you will have hope. Aians have two lives. You are not like us."

Oh, for a long time, I had forgotten that I was an Aian and I had two lives that I could live, which means that I can die for two times.

I didn't say a word. Cathy and Lowell stared at both of us, looking frightened.

"Come on, guys," Lowell first opened his mouth. "Don't fight. We should cooperate with each other throughout the quest. Charles, please accept how Adela feels. I totally understand her guilty feelings. You should try to understand."

I looked at Charles and our eyes met. He seemed to think for a moment and smiled.

"All right. I am so sorry for giving you a lot of pressure. I will try to make it easy for you when we all get to Elsmiere, I promise. But, please cheer up Adela. It makes me feel…sad looking at your gloomy face."

My heart jumped. I don't know why, but my face blushed red. I turned around from him and kept walking and walking.

For lunch, we sat by the hill and the trees and ate some tomato soup. It reminded me of Jeff's red face as I ate the soup. Lowell noticed me and tapped me gently on my shoulder.

"It's okay, Adela," he told me. "You will get over with it soon. It is not your fault, and no one can do anything about it. Try forgetting it."

I listened to what Lowell said to me, and closed my eyes. Forget what you did in Devina. Forget what you did with Jeff, no actually forget Jeff... but what if I forget about him and he waits for me to come?

Then suddenly, Cathy clicked her fingers. "No, Adela. That would be kind of hard. Maybe you should think optimistic, like Charles."

Okay, let me do what Cathy says. Hmm, there was nothing I could do because taking the throne is more important than friendship, I guess. And maybe I feel sorry for Jeff because he loves me so much and I had to refuse him.

"I feel much better," I lifted my head up and opened my eyes. "Thanks, guys. I will try to be optimistic."

Charles smiled. "Being optimistic can brighten up your future. I want you to remember that."

'Sure, I will. Thanks, Charles.' I thought.

Arrival

Elsmiere was very similar to what I expected. Elsmiere, the country that always blooms all over the place, was filled with lots and lots of flowers. Pansies, roses, daisies, clovers, you name them, they are all at Elsmiere.

Charles' face seemed to be lightened up a little bit. I was also little glad that Elsmiere was similar to Anastelon. Yay, I would finally get to eat all those royal best qualified foods in Elsmiere!

When we arrived there, there were many people greeting us. It was really odd that everyone was shaking a flower each instead of their flags.

"Why are they holding flowers?" I asked.

"Flowers are like the national flag of Elsmiere. They are showing how much they love flowers."

We got onto a carriage and the horses started to walk down the street.

Everyone cheered, "Salutations Ms. Monette and her lovely friends!"

Charles waved at those people. I decided to wave at them too. Then, Cathy and Lowell started to wave wildly with their both arms and shouted, "Hoo! Thanks everyone! Have a good day!"

The carriage stopped and we all get down on the ground. I stared at the big wide castle standing in front of me.

"Wow," I whispered. "It is even bigger than ours. It's incredible."

Charles chuckled. "You didn't even check out the inside. When you go in, everything would look just like your castle."

The speaker and the microphone got turned on. We looked up the stairs where the royals were. A man started to speak on the microphone.

"Ahem, welcome back his highness, Prince Jones!"

Everyone clapped and Charles turned around and waved at them.

"And greetings for our lovely guests, Ms. Monette who is the princess of Anastelon, and her friends, Mr. Henderson and Ms. Middleton."

We all turned around and waved at them. I smiled at those hundreds of people waving flowers.

"And now, would you please come up the stairs?" The man made gestures to us to come up the stairs.

We all climbed up the stairs and people kept on clapping and cheering from behind. We were ushered into the entrance and the door closed right behind us.

"What are we going to do right now?" I asked quietly.

"You guys will meet only our mother and my sister, since my father is off to Anastelon. My mother is called Queen Georgina and my sister is called Princess Olivianna. They are both kind, so you don't have to worry about anything, just be polite as much as you can be." Charles whispered at us as we entered the wide guestroom where all the knights, maids and the queen and the princess were. I swallowed.

We all stopped and Charles walked forward and vowed in front of Queen Georgina and Princess Olivianna. They were both so elegant and beautiful in their colorful dresses.

"Mother, I brought my companies along for Miss Adela Beth Monette's quest fulfillment. Would you allow her to learn the fighting skills while staying in Elsmiere?"

I could see he was asking her mother for allowance for us to stay here. The queen glanced at all of us and smiled gently.

"Yes, I allow all of you to stay here and train yourself the skills that you need for the quest."

Yay! We got permission from her! I cheered quietly inside.

"Ms. Adela Monette and Ms. Catherine Middleton, please come here. You may change into formal dresses before we have dinner."

The maid called Barbara ushered us into a wide room. When we entered the room, I couldn't keep my mouth shut. There were hundreds of closets and lots of shiny mirrors along the walls. Also, there were many women with velvet violet uniforms with their hair tied up in buns.

"Welcome to our beauty project room." One of the women said, and took my hand. Another woman took Cathy's hand and we were separated.

"My name is Naomi and I am here to decorate you!"

Naomi giggled and I let out a laugh. She seemed like she was really lively and outgoing. I liked her tone and the mood, which cheered me up from the tiring quest.

"Okay, sure. Please decorate me as beautiful as I could be." I said, giggling.

"Of course, so, what kinds of style do you like, do you like…well…let me think."

She touched my hair and swooped it around and tried making it in a bun, lopsided ponytail, and many ways she could find. Then, suddenly she squealed in joy and clicked her fingers.

"Oh, your highness! You fit nicely with the style of sexy and feminine. I should decorate you with that."

What? Oh my god, I swore to myself I don't fit the sexy style. How could she figure me out in such strange way? This is impossible.

"Let me first choose you a dress. Just a second."

Naomi disappeared into closet room and I sighed and looked myself in the mirror. Then I imagined myself wearing a showy and sexy dress. Ugh, I shivered.

"Oh, here it is! It will fit perfectly on you!" Naomi shouted from the closet. I stared at the closet until she came out, holding a red shiny strapless dress with jangling laces all over in the bottom. I shivered inside in pain. I wonder how much Cathy and Lowell would laugh when I appeared in front of them with this wild dress.

"Wow," I murmured in shock. "That looks so…wildly stunning to me."

"What do you mean, miss? Don't you like it?"

"Um," I shrugged and held up the dress in front of me. I stared at myself in the mirror, still in shock and fear. "I…love it, Naomi. You have a sense of fashion."

"Definitely," She said and clicked her fingers. "Now, get changed in that dressing room. It's right over there."

I went inside the dressing room and sighed to myself.

"I've never worn any dress like this." I muttered to myself and started changing my clothes. Then I finished wearing it in about 10 minutes and came out.

Naomi was standing right next to the dressing room. She saw me and squealed just like a kid who just earned a lollipop.

"Oh my goodness, miss, you look gorgeous just like the Goddess Hera. Do you know?"

"Oh, you mean, the Goddess of envy, Juno?" I lifted my head up. "Sure, I learned it from history class, but I am not sure how you know the Goddess Juno looked like."

"Well," she smiled as gentle as she could. "I meant you look just so beautiful. Now, we don't have much time for chitchats. I need you to get back to the chair and choose the hair style that you want."

All right. Now I get to choose.

I sat back in my chair and right behind me, Naomi came along with a magazine and handed it over to me.

"Here, this is the section for sexy concept. Choose one that you want and call me okay? I will be back quick."

Then Naomi walked swiftly to other room. I focused on the magazine that she gave to me. Oh my god, those hairstyles were so wild and unrealistic.

"Uh, what should I do?" I sighed and flipped the page, and found the hairstyle that I always wanted to try.

"Naomi?" I called her in my loud voice. "I chose it."

"All right," She came along in few seconds and leaned over me to check what I chose. I swallowed and pointed what I wanted.

Naomi smiled big. "Okay, so you want to braid one strip of your hair and tie it around your head like this and decorate your hair with the ribbon? Sure, but it kind of gets out of the point of sexiness. Is that okay?"

I nodded. So, Naomi started to braid one side of my hair and tie it around my head. Then she turned on the curling machine and started to curl my hair. After that, she took out a long black silky ribbon from her pocket and started to tie it around my hair in complicated way.

Time flew and finally, Naomi was done with my hair after she sprayed some cologne on the head. It smelled just like my mother, the scent of the flower Jasmine.

"Now, you are all done. Oh, wait. I almost forgot. I will bring the shoes for you."

Naomi hurriedly went off to a room again and grabbed a pair of peach colored stilettos and put them in front of me. The sharp points of the heels looked scary as if they were about to poke me. But I tried them on. They fit me perfectly.

"So, I am all done, right? Thanks for everything Naomi. I love my outfit. See you later." I waved at Naomi and walked away.

"Wait a second, miss," Naomi called me again. I looked around.

"I never allow anyone to wear this kind of necklace, but since you are the most gorgeous princess I have ever seen, I will let you wear it. Turn around for a second, will you?"

I turned around. I felt the cold feeling of silver touching my neck. Behind me, Naomi helped me lock the necklace. The touch of cold silver slithered around my neck.

"There you go," Naomi smiled. "You are the first person to wear this, so be careful with it."

Naomi ushered me to the front of a huge mirror. In the mirror, there was a tall girl wearing a short red dress, heels, and a beautiful silver emerald necklace. It was so beautiful.

"Wow," I murmured. "Thanks a lot. I really like the necklace. But, Naomi, why didn't you let anyone to wear this beautiful necklace except me?"

Naomi's smile disappeared. She did not look at me straight and seemed like she was busy.

"Um, I don't know why. I am just following what her majesty, Queen Georgina said from long time ago. But she allowed me to choose just one person to wear this necklace, so I chose you. You are the first and the last person to wear that beautiful necklace. Sad, isn't it?"

I stared at the necklace for a long time and whispered. "But why? I just…want to know why only one person gets to wear this necklace."

Naomi shrugged. "I have no idea about that. Oh, you are late. You should hurry. The dinner is going to be in just a few minutes."

My stomach rumbled as I patiently waited for the food to come out. There was only silence filling the air. Queen Georgina stood up and smiled with her gentle and tapped her glass cup with her tiny spoon. The glass rang across the room and soon everyone focused towards the Queen.

"Welcome everyone," The Queen said. "Today is a special day and we will be having a special dinner with our guests. And we..."

I don't really remember what she said that time, because I was starving to death! Gosh, I was sick and tired of hearing all the introductions and speeches before having meals. Also, it was way over dinner time. I kept on seeking the kitchen until the food came out, and as soon as the Queen sat down, dozens of waiters came out with lots of dishes and bowls.

"Smell so good, don't they?" Cathy leaned over me and whispered.

"Shhh!"

"...and we will have our wonderful and fulfilling dinner party starting now."

Queen Georgina tapped the glass cup with her spoon for three times. I swallowed as hundreds of dishes and plates landed on the table. I couldn't stop staring at them, since I had never eaten food like I'd eaten in Anastelon. I had been hoping Elsmiere's delicacy is similar as Anastelon's.

However surprisingly, every one of the plates looked so familiar. They were all kinds of foods I had eaten back in the castle!

My mouth made a shape of an 'o'. My eyes automatically turned to the Queen and our eyes met.

"I specially ordered the chefs to cook the delicacy that you usually ate back in your country." She smiled. "I understand how you would miss the food from your country. I hope the taste is similar."

I took a sip of the mushroom soup. Mmmm…it exactly reminded me of the soup I ate back in Anastelon. I had never felt so happy like this before.

"Wow," I took a lot spoonful of the soup and kept on eating. "That's very nice of you. It feels like home eating this soup. Thank you so much, your majesty."

I finished eating the soup in just seconds. I felt Olivianna staring at me since I was eating too fast and voraciously. It made the stress and the fatigue disappear. It felt so stabilized and peaceful inside. I was surprised how I was too much accommodated with Anastelon.

As I put down the bowl, I glanced at my friends eating their soup. Charles was slowly eating the soup, and Cathy and Lowell were devouring so fast as if they were going to eat the whole table.

As soon as the bowls were all empty, the waiters took away the bowls and placed a meatloaf for each one of us. The smell of roasted garlic and savory yams tickled my nostrils. I took a deep breath and lifted the knife and the fork. Then I dived in and squished the food into my mouth as fast as I could. I cut the juicy steak and pushed it into my mouth and chewed just a few times. I felt a huge chunk of meat rolling down my throat, but I was hoping it would lower my hunger.

"It seems that Miss Adela is having a contest of who is the speediest eater between her companions." Queen Georgina murmured, but it echoed loudly since it was all silent.

I stopped moving the fork and lifted my head up. Uh oh, manners. I forgot everything about manners. How stupid I am. It's been only about a week and I forgot everything I had been doing everyday at home. I can't believe it.

I could feel my face turn scarlet as I felt every person in that room staring at me. The silence filled the air as Cathy and Lowell also stopped devouring the food.

Next time, I will never ever forget my manners! I decided.

Olivianna

It was my first night staying in Elsmiere and I felt so much comfortable sleeping in a similar place as my castle. The room had a soft clean comfy bed with lots of cushions, and a wide bathroom where I could take showers and baths everyday and whenever I wanted. It felt like heaven to me.

That night I took a long shower and I loved the aroma of the cleansing soaps and shampoo. When I got out from the bathroom and lay down on the bed, I heard a short knock on the door.

Hmm, who would it be? I wondered and walked cautiously toward the door. I opened and saw Olivianna standing with her bare feet. She was wearing a dress pajama made with silky pink fabric.

"Olivianna," I whispered and looked around the hallway checking if anyone's out. "Why are you here? Is there anything you want to tell me sweetie?"

"Um," Her shoulders shuddered as she looked over at me. I could feel the chilly wind swishing through my bones. "I just wanted to join in…"

"Join in where?"

"…"

She was twisting her legs shyly. Maybe it is better to take her inside, I thought.

"Come inside sweetheart. It is really cold outside." I gently tugged Olivianna inside and closed the door. Then I pulled her hand toward the sofa. We both sat down facing each other with a small tea table between us. I could see she was still twisting her bodies and not looking at me straight. I thought of an idea to get her comfortable.

"Hey," I smiled as kindly as I could. She lifted her head up slowly and stared at me with her dark brown eyes. "Do you want some hot chocolate? I think I remember seeing it on the cupboard."

She nodded and smiled with her cute teeth. So I ran to the cupboard, boiled the water and took out two mugs and made two cups of sweet hot chocolate. It smelled so sweet as if it would melt me.

I brought the cups of hot chocolate to the tea table and put down the cup right in front of Olivianna. She smiled again and held up the cup carefully and said, "Thank you very much Miss Monette."

I smiled. "Call me Adela. I like it that way."

Again, she kept on smiling, showing her white teeth. Then I realized that her skin color was dark and her hair was black unlike her family. It was strange. Charles and Queen Georgina were blonde and King Jones had ginger brown hair and only Olivianna looked so different not like her family.

"Sweetie," I said. "Why do you look different from your family?"

Her body suddenly got hardened. She did not say a word. She looked as if she became a hard rock. Her smile disappeared and looked as if she was about to cry.

"No, no, darling, don't you cry like that. Why are you feeling depressed all so sudden, huh? Is it because you can't answer me?"

She knocked her head down as she dropped her tears into her pajamas.

I sat next to her and hugged her gently. "Please don't cry. You don't have to tell me if you don't want to. It's too late. Do you want me to bring you to your room, Olivianna?"

She did not answer, but she sobbed on and on. I asked myself what to do, and decided to tuck her in my bed and sleep together.

I lifted her and brought her to my bed. I carefully put her down on the right side of my bed and laid a sheet of blanket over her body. Olivianna stopped crying and stared at me with her watery dark eyes.

"Good night princess. Tonight we can sleep together. I will be right beside you."

I kissed her forehead and turned out all the lights except the lamp beside the bed. I was worried if she was afraid of the dark. Then I lay down beside Olivianna. My eyelids started to feel heavy. But before I went to sleep, I checked on Olivianna for the last time.

I could see her sleeping peacefully. I felt relieved and went to sleep.

"Where's Olivianna? She is gone!"

I woke up when I heard a roar echoing through the hall in the early morning. I rubbed my eyes and got out of bed. Oh, wait. I needed to check on Olivianna. I turned and looked at her side. But she was not there. All there left was a piece of blanket that she used yesterday night.

Suddenly, there was a knock on the door. I swallowed and opened it.

There was a maid standing in front of the door, looking so nervous.

"Your Highness, good morning. I am so sorry for disturbing your gracious morning, but have you seen Princess Olivianna?"

"Oh my god," I mumbled and looked around my room. "Actually um… what's your name may I ask?"

"It's Hannah, your Highness."

"Hannah," I took a deep breath and looked around the room again. "I need to tell you something."

"Yes, your Highness."

"Um, actually Princess Olivianna came to my room last night."

Hannah's eyes got bigger and her mouth made a shape like an 'o'.

"Oh, did she? Then where is our princess? Is she here right now?"

"No no, I am not sure. She had slept right beside me last night, but she was gone when I woke up in the morning."

"Jesus Christ! Everyone in our castle is all looking for her. We need to find her fast or Queen Georgina will call the security."

"Is Charles awake?"

"Do you mean Prince Jones jr.? Of course he is. He wakes up at 5, miss. He is an early bird. Now I think he is looking for her sister as well."

I sighed. "Hmm, okay let me guess. The windows…are not open, so she would not have escaped through the windows. Um, maybe she would have escaped by the door or maybe she is still here…I think."

"Achoo!" There was a small sound coming from my closet. Hannah and I ran to the closet and slammed opened it. As I expected, Olivianna was sitting there, hiding.

"Oh my princess!" Hannah grabbed her hand and pulled her out strongly. "Where have you been? Bad girl."

I could see her face covered with tears. Her eyes were red from crying too much.

"Olivianna…"I wanted to ask her why she was crying, but I stopped because it may make her cry more.

"Let's go missy. It's already about 9 and everyone still did not have breakfast yet because of you, bad girl."

Hannah grabbed Olivianna's hand and walked straight outside. Olivianna kept on looking back at me with her eyes begging for help, but since I did not know why she was crying, I couldn't not help her. Before Hannah closed the door, she spinned around and curtsied.

"Please forgive us for so many troubles. I will make sure that Princess Olivianna does not disturb you ever again. Please be ready for breakfast in 30 minutes, miss, and come down the stairs to where you ate dinner yesterday. Thank you."

Hannah disappeared so quickly down the hall. I heard footsteps echo through the hall. I sighed and opened the closet to choose what to wear, but I still couldn't stop thinking about Olivianna. Why did she come to my room last night? Why did she cry when I ask her why she looked different? What did her mournful looks mean? Is there something that she is hiding?

I grabbed a medium sized lime colored dress and kept on thinking and thinking.

The breakfast was okay-ish. There were two sausages, scrambled eggs, Caesar salad, and so on, but they were not that good as I thought. The salad was slimy, and fried eggs were cold. I thought it was because it was way over breakfast time. The whole time, I was staring at both Charles and Olivianna. Gosh, I wanted to know what was going on between Olivianna and her family.

After eating the most disgusting and awkward breakfast, I was told to wear comfortable clothes for dynamic movements. So I grabbed leggings and a t-shirt from the closet and put them on. I tied my long hair up in a ponytail and went straight downstairs to the garden.

When I opened the door of the garden, I could see so many flowers in front of me. There were white, blue, red, yellow, any color you think of. The petals flew with the wind and tickled my nostrils with its wonderful smell. I kept on walking as I counted all the flowers in this enormous garden. One two three…it was up to millions I thought.

"Quite beautiful eh?" Charles appeared from behind. I looked around the garden and nodded. "Yeah, I love it. It's so beautiful."

"It has been more than 200 years keeping this garden," Charles said. "The flowers grew and bloomed and they drooped. Then we would plant other flowers. The process has been circulating until now."

"That's really amazing."

"Yeah, I know. We even call this garden our treasure. My father loves this garden so much. I dare call this garden 'a source of pride'. Now, do you know why we are here, Adela?"

I shrugged. "I don't know. Why are we here?"

"We are going to stay here for weeks for you to learn some fighting skills."

Oh my god, what did he just say?

"It would be very hard for you to learn dozens of skills, but I am willing to teach you with my full responsibility. I am not an Aian like you, but I studied about Aians a month before the quest, so it may not be too hard."

"Wait, wait," This is too complicated. I could not arrange my thoughts since he gave me too much shock. "So you are saying that I need to learn skills from you and fight the evils by myself?"

"I will help you in the actual war. Also, there will be soldiers from Elsmiere, so you don't have to worry too much…"

"I am leaving." I interrupted and turned around from him. I can't do this. This is too much for me. It was so hard for me to walk for miles and now they are asking for me to fight hundreds of enemies with those unstable skills? Wake up that is totally impossible. My father must have gone out of mind.

Suddenly I felt a strong grip on my shoulders. He turned me around. His face looked red and furious.

"Adela Beth Monette!" He called. "Stop escaping from reality! This is your real life and you have no choice but to learn the skills."

"But it's…"

"It is too hard for you? Okay I get it. I never knew you were that weak to accept the mission."

"I am not weak Charles!" I shouted. "I am just…well…"

I knocked my head down and sighed.

"You are too afraid of yourself Adela," Charles murmured. "Please listen to what I tell you to do. Please, Adela, for yourself and everyone around you."

I hesitated. But, what if I die in the war? I asked myself. Why do I have to fight in the war?

"Okay, I will do it." I grabbed a sword and faced Charles. Charles looked stunned at first, but he smiled and grabbed his sword.

"These swords aren't real, so they don't hurt if you hit your body with these. I am first going to see how you can treat the sword. Let's start!"

I felt my heart beat so loudly in anxiousness. I swallowed and started swinging the sword madly and quickly as I could, so that he would be surprised at my unexpected actions. As I expected, his eyes widened and he was stunned to see me moving the sword madly.

But, as I move around the sword really quick, Charles avoided my sword and started to join in the fight.

Two swords hit each other making 'clinging' sounds. My head felt like spinning, so I just moved my sword around as fast as I could so Charles would not be able to see the sword flying all over the place.

I am so good, I thought, but when I started to gain self-confidence, Charles' face started to get twisted and distorted. Then suddenly, he started laughing his head off and fell off to the ground, grabbing his stomach. I stopped swishing my sword around and stared at him confused.

"Why are you laughing?" I asked. But Charles kept on laughing and laughing for minutes. Then he stopped and calmed himself down.

"Gosh Adel, didn't you see yourself? You...you were swinging your sword so crazily...and that was so...ha ha!"

My mind went blank. I could feel my face burn and about to steam out.

Did he just laugh at me? I thought as I was blushing.

Charles laughed and laughed until he saw my face turn into a frown.

"I am sorry," He apologized. "I was laughing because you were being so...crazy and lunatic!"

"What???" my jaw dropped. "What do you mean? I...I was just trying to..."

Charles coughed several times to stop laughing and being so rude in front of me. Gosh, he is so rude! This is terrible. This was the weirdest and the worst experience I had with him and I couldn't stop frowning.

Finally he noticed that I was feeling really upset.

"Adela," He sighed and begged. "I am so sorry for being so rude.

I promise it'll never happen again. I forgot that you were new to everything..."

"Oh yeah? Well, you shouldn't have."

I spinned around and dropped the sword. I walked swiftly through the door and into the castle. I heard running footsteps behind me and a powerful grip held my shoulder.

"Ouch" I gritted my teeth. Charles turned me and grabbed both of my shoulders with his tense expression on his face.

"I told you I am sorry," He said slowly, pushing down his anger. "So would you please just..."

"No, I don't want to." I tried to turn away from him, but he grabbed my shoulders with more strength.

"It was very thoughtless of me to act like that, so would you please listen to me?" He sighed and looked straight into my eyes. "Please?"

His voice croaked, and we stared at each other for a long time.

Then I glanced at the servants behind Charles, signing with his hands to accept Charles.

I sighed. "All right, I am being very thoughtful right now. Show me how you can do it then. I swear I will stop learning if that happens again next time."

Charles smiled and grabbed my hands tight. "Let's do it then."

The owls started weeping through the darkness. It was already very late at night and I realized that I had practiced with Charles for about 7 hours or so. I waved good bye to Charles and walked across the field and spotted Cathy standing beside one of the arches in front of the door, waiting for me.

"Hey," I tapped Cathy's shoulder and grinned, but she wasn't smiling as the way she does. "Hey, Cathy. Let's go."

I realized she was staring into the spaces, daydreaming. Why is she acting so strangely?

"Cathy, Cathy?" I shook her shoulder strongly until she looked back at me and said, "What?"

"Cathy," I frowned. "What happened to you? Is there something wrong?"

"Well," She sighed and looked at me as if she was about to burst into tears. She swallowed her lump in her throat and croaked out the shocking words.

"Lowell loves you."

Lowell

"What?" I gasped and could not say a word. "Wait, do you mean he loves me as a friend or like a crush?"

"Definitely like a crush."

"But how can you be so sure?" I snorted. "Is there any evidence?"

"Of course there is evidence." She shouted with her voice full of sorrow and worry. She sighed and stared at me blankly. I could see her love for Lowell. She was crushing on him so hard that I could almost feel her heartache.

"Tell me then." I calmed myself.

Cathy slowly walked towards the bench across the hallway where we could see the views of the garden. She sat there and signed to me to come over. "Come here," She murmured. "Sit."

I sat. I could hear the wind blow from outside. I shivered and felt goosebumps running down my back. I rubbed my hands and arms and gritted my teeth.

"I feel the weather is still cold even in the spring." Cathy mumbled and smiled. I looked at her and I swore I knew she was crying in the insides. I kept wondering, but how? How could Lowell love me? I thought we were just friends.

"Please tell me, Catherine." I begged.

Cathy seemed like she didn't want to let it out, or remind herself of it.

"Uh well, have you spotted Lowell staring at you while you were learning from Charles?"

"What do you mean?" I squinted.

"Lowell had been staring at you for like, 6 hours or so, sitting on this bench. I saw him when I was walking the hallway. So I tapped him and asked. "What are you doing?" and he did not even look at me. He was like, staring into the spaces…and he looked so tense. I followed his eyes and noticed that he was staring at both of you. I tapped him and shook him to wake him out of his daydream, and he turned at me, surprised.

He was like, "Hey, what's up?" and I could tell that he was staring at you the whole time. I swear he had been."

I snorted. "You can't be so sure about this Cathy. You are being too sensitive and obsessive all over him. I mean think about you these days. You cannot get your eyes off of him. You should give yourself a rest, Cathy."

"But you didn't see him. You should have seen him…I mean he was looking at you for hours. Who would do that really? Staring at one person for 7 hours without any movements? That's ridiculous."

"Hmm…" I thought about the reason why he was acting like that. Nothing popped up in my head. I thought and thought, but more I thought about it, it made me get careless about his acts.

"Come on Cathy, just chill yourself. It was just one day. I am pretty sure he was just enjoying the nice breeze and the sunlight and all these wonderful views of this garden. I would do that if I was him."

"But…well…all right. Let's see about that tomorrow then." Cathy sighed and dropped her head. Aww, I hugged her tightly and rubbed my hand on her backs.

"Don't you worry about that Cathy. I am always seeking to help you stay close. But you should not be so shy when you're with him. You're always like a scared little girl in front a wolf. You should be self-confident. Boys like that kind of reaction from girls."

"I know…I know…" She rubbed her hands on my back and stood up from the bench. "Let's go."

Many days had passed and I had learned about 10 skills of using swords from Charles. Also it made me kind of nervous if Lowell was staring at me behind the arches like Cathy told me, but the day after she told me, I couldn't see him when I checked. Charles told me to concentrate whenever I glanced at the arches. Then I just laughed it off and continued fighting with him.

The greatest thing that I like it here was that I was able to talk during meal time. I could chitchat with my friends, mostly Cathy and Charles. I felt so far away from Lowell these days. He didn't talk much, but I did not really care because he was always like that. He would rather be quiet and read books.

But I suddenly became curious. "Hey." I called Lowell, sitting diagonally from where I was. He looked up.

"Uh, yeah?"

"I haven't seen you these days. Where have you been?"

Lowell seemed surprised and flustered. "Um, well you know while you're doing your stuff, I am doing mine."

"Hmm, okay." I nodded and turned to Cathy. "You told me you were learning flowers from the gardener. How's all the flower studies."

"Uh, it's called horticulture, to be specific. I enjoy it so much. It is even great to learn it by experience. I feel like when I get back to Anastelon, I would get 100% on Ecology, especially the flower parts."

"Oh, really? That's just great Cathy!"

And of course, I noticed Lowell was hiding something. I had to find out.

Stalker

Strange, Lowell never had acted like that before. I kept checking on Lowell every second and realized he was twitching his eyebrows awkwardly, just like when he lies. Then he slipped away from the party so naturally so no one could notice him.

I need to follow him, I thought.

I stared at where he was heading and turned to my friends.

"Hey guys, I think I left something in the dining room. I will go get it. You guys can go."

When I waved at them and turned away, Charles grabbed my wrist.

"Do you want me to come with you?" He asked.

I smiled and shook my head gently. Charles shrugged and walked down the hall with Cathy.

I swiftly ran toward the way where Lowell headed and I could hear his footsteps ringing through the hall.

He went...this way, I quickly decided and ran down the hall and saw Lowell standing in front of a small gate, struggling to find the right key to open it.

He was holding like dozens of keys, clinging onto one ring. Where did he get those keys? I wondered and waited until he found the right key.

He repeated to put the key, try to turn it and pull it out and try another one.

When he repeated that for about 14 times, he had the lock unlocked.

"Yes!" He whispered and quietly opened the door. The gate slid open and the room was filled with darkness. He stepped inside and turned on the lights. I could peer inside through the gap and saw hundreds of bookshelves all in straight rows. It was a library.

Whoa, I whispered and stepped toward the gate. Maybe I should sneak inside and see what it is like, I thought.

But suddenly, just as I was about to enter the library, the gate was loudly shut. Oh god, did Lowell just closed the door? That made my heart jump!

I sighed and pushed the door as quietly as possible. But the door was too heavy that it didn't move an inch. I pushed harder. Uh oh, why isn't it opening? I leaned against the door and pushed as hard as I could, but the door did not even move. Shit, I grumbled.

"What are you doing there?" I heard a voice behind me and I stood there, frozen.

I felt chills running through my neck. It was one of Charles' closest guards. I've seen him before a few times, but I couldn't remember his name. It was J… something.

"This is a private library for, Prince Jones," He said. "You shouldn't be entering this library, your highness."

I thought fast. "But, well…wait. What was your name? Was it Jo…?"

"It is Jonathan, your highness."

"Oh, yes. Jonathan. I am ordering you to open this gate for me and my words are solid."

"But miss, this is Prince Jones' private place. He never allows anyone to enter…"

"Well, he actually allowed me to enter the library." I lied. Wow, I couldn't believe that those fake words could come out of my mouth so naturally. I tried to keep my face still so he wouldn't know that I was lying.

He looked surprised. "Did he? Are you sure about that your highness?"

"Of course I am sure. Now tell me how to open the door quick. I am kind of struggling right now."

Jonathan came closer and glanced at the unlocked lock hanging onto the door. He seemed confused.

"Why is the door unlocked miss?" He asked. "I am known that the library key is hidden and hard to find according to the Prince. How did you open the gate may I ask?"

I brain spinned fast and made up quick fake words again. "Um well, Charles told me that he visited the library before dinner…and maybe he forgot to lock it."

Jonathan seemed doubtful, but he helped me open the door. I realized that the door that I was pushing was unmovable. The other one was what I had to push. Shame on me.

"Thanks Jonathan, I will see you later." I waved at him stepped inside the library.

The library was so quiet and I could not even hear a thing. Where is

Lowell? I wondered and looked around the humongous room filled with millions of books on the shelves.

I looked over the titles of some of the books that caught my eye.

'Nature in Time'

'Love of Lives'

'Fallacious Testimony'

'All about Elsmiere QnAs'

Most of them were thick like dictionary book, but those catchy titles made me want to read them more, so I grabbed one of them and started reading.

I stood there for a long time, not able to get my eyes off of the book. I found the writer of that book was a famous man that I have known.

I read through the pages and found myself focused, so focused that I couldn't even hear Lowell call my name.

"Hey, is that you Adela?" He shook my shoulder. I looked up at him and jumped.

"Oh my god! I am terribly sorry." I quickly closed the book. Lowell seemed disconcerted for a second, and then he laughed off.

"What? What are you sorry for Adela?"

"Well, sorry for stalking you maybe?"

Lowell grunted and smiled. "Nah, it's okay. I heard someone pushing on the doors for few times and I thought I was caught by those guards! I felt so relieved that it was you Adela. If I have gotten caught, I would have been dead!"

I giggled. "Well, as long as we stick together, you're not dead. They wouldn't dare to kill a princess, would they?"

We both laughed and had a nice chat. We hardly had had any chats since we came to Elsmiere. So it felt pretty good to talk and make jokes with him. I laughed hard and felt so happy that Lowell was back.

"Are you feeling okay about your school works back in Anastelon?"

I carefully asked and looked at his face. But he grinned and shrugged.

"Well, I feel better than before," he said. "Actually I feel happy for you Adela, and I like the fact that I am helping you to receive the throne."

"Aww," I smiled. "Thanks for coming with me on this quest. Without you, or without Cathy, nothing would have worked out."

"Nah, Charles is the one who takes the most parts. You know, he teaches us everything. I can infer that he has been reading a lot of nature books from this library."

Then I suddenly realized the strange thing and asked, "Hey, I am wondering, how did you get the keys?"

Lowell became stiff and seemed as he was stuck. He rolled his eyes around as if he did not have any idea how to explain it. Then he slowly opened his mouth.

"You should swear to God that you will never ever open your mouth about this." He whispered and leaned over to me. I nodded and zipped my mouth.

He chuckled and whispered, "Well, it may sound kind of mean, but when you and Charles practiced the sword skills, I was curious about the structure of this castle, so I sort of explored all of those thousands of rooms in the castle. I could see the castle was huge and sometimes I couldn't find my way back to my room,"

Oh, I nodded. That's what he's been doing.

"And one day I found Charles' room," he looked to his left and right to be sure that no one else was listening. "And there were even no guards or maids, so I secretly sneaked inside his room to see what it looked like."

"How was it?" I interrupted and giggled quietly.

Lowell sniggered. "It was very big, just like your room Adela. There was nothing much different from your room. He had lots of trophies from sword fight competitions. Also, he had some awards of best student in class."

I nodded and Lowell kept on talking.

"Anyway, I know this is mean, but I was so curious. Well, I searched through some of the drawers of his. Then I found these keys. I was curious, so I stole them."

"When did you steal them?"

"Well, last Friday right before dinner."

I knew Lowell has gone out his mind. How could he steal Charles' key?

"Hey you know what?" He sighed and laughed to himself. "I have no idea how to put this back to Charles."

Oh my god, he must have really gone out of his mind.

"What?" I gasped in horror. "This is…just horrible. I mean, this is stealing Lowell. How could you think of this?"

"I don't really know, Adela. I was so curious…and I wanted to enter the library." He replied absentmindedly. Now what should I do… If he gets kicked out or sent to jail, we all would be in so much trouble. Even worse, if my father knows this, he may not be allowed to go to prestigious university.

"What are you going to do Lowell? This is…well this is terrible. This is totally stealing. You may go to jail, or you would get punished. Or even worse, it would be unable for you to enter the university that you want to go. Didn't you think of that when you stole that key from the drawer?"

Lowell's face hardened and looked as if he had no idea.

"Maybe you can help me out. You can tell Charles that I was sent to his room to look for something and I accidently took the key."

"Well but, how could you accidently grab the key without knowing it? That's ridiculous! I think it is better to say the truth, don't you think?"

"No!" He screamed in shock and shivered. "Charles wouldn't understand. It is so obvious that I stole it!"

"Then what should we do? What should we do?" I was in a dither.

However, Charles did not look as nervous as I was. He rather looked so pleasant and even shuffled his eyes through the books. Then he suddenly clicked his fingers and grabbed my wrist.

"Hey, I have something to show you. Follow me." He pulled. But I pulled back.

"Uh uh," I shook my head. "We shouldn't play around here. We should get out of here as quick as possible. Follow me."

"No. Adela, follow me. I found something so cool. It may make you get shocked."

Lowell pulled my arm with more force and dragged me along the way. I hissed. "Stop it! We are going to get in so much trouble."

"We are already in so much trouble." Lowell suddenly stopped in front of the huge bookshelf. It was filled with lots of difficult and thick books (mostly about economics) and I certainly didn't want to read them.

I glanced at Lowell. "Why are we here? Are you going to recommend me a book again Lowell? If you are, I certainly am not interested in those weird boring..."

"Ah, here it is." He picked a book that was placed at his eyelevel. 'The Silence of the Darks' it read. The cover of the book was made of turquoise silk and it was ever so clean unlike other books on the shelf. The title was knitted on the cover so neatly.

"Here," Lowell handed the book to me. "I recommend you to read it. You'll find it quarry."

"Huh," I squinted. "I am not that interested in this kind of things. Besides, why are you recommending this to me Lowell?"

"You'll see about that." Lowell chuckled and walked by me.

"Hey wait! What should I do with this book?" I asked.

"Just read it silly!" Lowell stopped walking and turned around. He saw me standing frozen.

"Come on let's go." Lowell pulled my hand again.

"Whoa." We were out of the library faster than a blink. Then Lowell locked the door as fast as he could as I stood there, still frozen.

As he finished locking, he smiled at me. I quickly woke myself up from daydreaming.

"Wha...what is this all about Lowell? You are just...this is...stealing you know. This is too obvious. You just made the evidence."

"Nope, we are not stealing. We are borrowing from Charles."

"Why are you being so stubborn Lowell? You are annoying sometimes."

I screamed in shock, but Lowell didn't even seem distracted. He just laughed to himself and waved goodbye.

PART 2

Lowell

"Whenever I look at you,
my whole heart freezes.
Whenever you look at me,
the whole world freezes."

Can Boys and Girls be Friends?

Yeah, just like the title, I am wondering. Can boys and girls be friends? Well, my answer is; definitely no. I've never ever thought about a female friend. I mean, boys and girls are totally different. Well, if a boy is gay, that would be an exception, but really, boys and girls always have an element called 'love' between them. Well, for example if a boy and a girl had been friends for like, 6 years or so, the friendship between them would sooner turn to the thoughts like, 'I can't live without him or her' and they would realize that the weird feeling is love. Boys exist for girls and girls exist for boys.

And I exist for Adela and Adela exists for me.

This is how I think about her. But she doesn't seem to realize. No one knows that I have a crush on her since I have been with her for 6 years and it feels like a tragedy to me. Her green sparkling eyes, natural brunette hair, beautiful lips, and rosy cheeks… She is just perfect. How could anyone hate her?

Anyway, this is just my feelings, not hers. I think she believes that boys and girls can be friends. It is the difference in our thinking that tears apart and makes us stay as friends. And I hate it so much.

I tried many things to show my love to her. I tried writing letters, but I couldn't send them to her because I wasn't brave enough. I also tried talking to her about how I actually feel, but we would always end up playing jokes on each other and laughing away. Nothing has ever worked really, and I always end up hating myself for it.

Sometimes I wonder what would happen if I really get braver and ask her out. Maybe she would accept me, or maybe she would just dump me and get disappointed at me for spoiling our friendship.

So the time flew and I kept my love inside for a long time until now. It has been 6 years for heaven's sake. I think it is time for her to recognize. But she never does.

I walked down the hallway and realized that I was still holding the key. I turned around and saw Adela still standing and thinking of what she'd do with the book. I came to her and slipped the key into her hand.

"There you go," I whispered quietly. "I am so sorry, but please do this for me. All right? You are the only one who could put it back without many doubts."

"But, how…" She couldn't continue on with her words.

"I don't know, but I will think about some ways." I whispered and walked away from her. "I am so sorry Adela. Please forgive me. I had never thought about the future."

But she looked so worried and she wouldn't move an inch. I sighed and opened my mouth with courage.

"Maybe… we could go together…to Charles' room." I said slowly.

Adela lifted her head up and smiled a little.

"That's much better."

I swallowed. Step by step, as slowly and carefully as I could, I tiptoed inside with Adela. She slowly closed the door behind us and glanced out the door to check if no one's watching. The door creaked behind her and she nodded at me.

"Go Lowell!" She whispered.

I swallowed and sighed in deep breath.

Okay, where did I find the key? Oh, yes. I think I picked it up from that drawer over there...

I sneaked toward the drawer with such colorful and elegant feature. Wait, it was not the drawer that I took the key from. I turned away from the drawer and searched around. There was another drawer behind the plants. I rushed to it and looked around the drawer to see if it was right. No, this was not it. I rushed to another drawer and checked if it was the one I was looking for. But it was not the one.

Strange, I thought. I definitely know how it looks, but I can't find it. It couldn't have run off by itself, could it?

"Why is it taking so long?" Adela hissed and stamped her feet.

"I just can't find the drawer. I exactly know how it looks like, but it isn't here!"

"What does it look like?" She asked nervously.

"It was dark brownish and it had a little scratch on the cover. It also had a white silk sheet over it as I recall."

I could feel my hand so wet in my sweat. Then I realized I was shivering in fear.

"Why don't you know where you got the key? You should have known where you got it from. That's so weird."

"I know, but I already checked the place I'd been to, but the drawer was so different from what I'd seen."

"That is nonsense! No one could have changed the drawer in such a short period. I mean, could have they remove the drawer and switch into a new one?"

"That could be a possibility, couldn't it?" I shrugged and ran to where I first checked. The drawer was completely white and it was so different from what I recall. Adela followed me and stood next to the drawer. I carefully opened it to check if it was empty and new. The drawer dragged open and it was filled with so many envelopes and postages. It was not the right one.

"Damn it," I hissed and looked around to see if there were any drawers that looked the same as I'd seen. Then I realized Adela was looking at the envelopes inside the drawer. Her face looked pale and her whole body froze. I followed her gaze and read the cover of the envelope.

It read,

'To Adela Monette
From your awaiting true friend, Thomson.'

Conflicts

"It is from Thomson," Adela whispered in shock. I stood there with my mouth open. "Jeffrey, it's from Jeffrey." She held up the envelope and smoothed the cover. She blew the dust away and slowly clicked open the envelope. A letter came out of the envelope and she flipped it open.

I couldn't move an inch as she read through the letter. I could see her eyes flutter and her hands tremble. Her eyes were filled up with tears as she finished reading the letter. She looked up at me as she dropped her tears.

"Jeffrey wrote to me. Oh my god...she put the letter on the top of the drawer and took out all the letters. I could see the envelopes and postages were countless. On every envelope, it said, 'To my sweet Adela, From Thomson'

Or along the lines of

'To my lovely lady, From Jeffrey'

"They are all for me!" Adela shouted in sorrow. "How come Charles has all my posts?"

"What are you guys doing?" A sharp voice rang through the room from the door. We both looked up and shivered.

Oh no, it was Charles, looking ever so furious.

He rushed across the room to where we were at and snatched away the envelopes from Adela.

"You don't deserve to read these stupid letters Miss Monette." He screamed madly. But Adela didn't let go of the letters.

"No, they are mine. How dare you call these letters stupid? Why are you keeping my letters inside your drawer?"

"Why are you sneaking into someone's room without an allowance?"

"They are mine Charles, give them back."

"No, you tell me first why these are here."

"What are you guys doing?" A high-pitched voice came from the door. It was Cathy.

Adela and Charles stopped pulling the envelopes. Cathy ran toward us and snatched the envelopes. She carefully read the words on the cover and looked at all of us.

"What happened? I mean, why are you guys fighting over Adela's posts? Why are you...?"

"I'll explain it to you later Cathy." Adela mumbled and snatched the envelopes away from Cathy. She lowered her head and walked away from us swiftly.

What should I do...what should I do... my mind was completely messed up and I didn't know what to do. I stared at Adela's back and I decided to chase her up.

I caught up with Adela and grabbed her shoulder.

"Adela, please just calm down. I think Charles has something to explain..."

"Explain? Explain what? I don't want to hear any explanations."

"Please, let's get back to Charles and see why he hid the letters."

Adela hesitated. Then she noticed that I was still holding the keys.

She smiled and slipped the keys to her fingers.

"This is it," She murmured.

Loud footsteps rang throughout the hall. We both looked up. There were Charles running toward us and behind him was Cathy, already out of breath.

"Okay, I will explain everything Adela," He blurted out quickly. "This Thomson guy is a jerk. He wrote about 35 letters to you in total. He is a stalker Adela. I read most of the letters, and they were…I mean he was out of mind. You don't have to read these letters. You'll never be able to meet him again as well."

"What do you mean I'll never be able to meet him? How dare you call him a jerk? He is such a nice boy. He is sending these many letters just because I didn't send him back."

"That's not all I said. I checked most of those letters and they were filled with disgusting and…well actually you don't need to hear about what they are all about. They are all rubbish. Also, he has quite a lot grammar and spelling mistakes. What a stupid boy he is."

Adela breathed in to rebut his words, but stopped. She folded her arms and held out her secret weapon; the keys.

"Uh oh, I am sorry that you haven't notice that your keys were taken."

Charles stared at the keys for a long time. Then his mouth dropped and shivered.

"Wait a minute! Why is that key...?"

Adela smiled and played the keys around her fingers.

But Charles shouted back furiously. "But when did you steal those keys?"

Adela hesitated for a second. I rolled my head fast as I could and snapped in their conversation.

"We took it right before you came in," I interrupted hurrily. "We were wondering about the key and then you burst in. That's what happened."

Charles sighed and shook his head like he had no idea. Adela smiled.

"How about a fair trade?" She suggested. "You give me all those envelopes and I give you the keys."

Charles hesitated for a minute and nodded slowly.

"All right. Give me the keys first."

"No, you give me the letters first."

"Stop stop stop guys! Give me those. I'll make it fair."

Cathy grabbed both envelopes and keys. Then she crossed her hands and handed Adela the envelopes and handed Charles the keys.

"Happy now?" She smiled as they both grabbed what they wanted.

Adela smiled for a second. Then her smile vanished and she glared at Charles sharply.

"I will always remember this, Charles" She said. "This was the first time you ever hid something away from me."

I'd never known what all those letters were all about, but I could feel how much Adela miss her friend Thomson. The day after that day, she appeared at the dining room with her eyes completely red. It was the first time I saw her roughly dressed. Her clothes were wrinkled and a little dirty, and her hair, which was always tied up in a bun neatly, was just roughly tied up in a ponytail. Everyone was surprised to see Adela like that since she loved to stay neat and clean as possible.

I carefully approached to her and sat right beside her.

"Good morning Adela," I started. "Did you have a hard time sleeping last night? Your eyes are all red."

Adela tried to smile and I could see just a tip of her mouth moving slightly up. She let out her breath and looked at me blankly.

"Well yeah, I guess..." She sighed and murmured.

"Are you all right? You look kind of sick. Maybe you should go see the doctor huh?" I said as I examined her eyes.

Adela shook her head. "No I am just fine. It was just a nightmare, that's all."

I know you read the letters overnight Adela, I wanted to say these words out loud, but I shut my mouth and sipped the tea from the table.

Adela took a sip, too and daydreamed. What happened to you Adela? What were those letters about? I wanted to ask so badly, but I had to keep quiet.

Cathy seemed worried, too. But she seemed to be decided that it was better not to talk to her in this situation.

A minute later, the door opened the breakfast was delivered by many servants and maids. On each plate, there were sausages, chicken salad, a boiled egg, waffle with syrup and a small apple pie which was Adela's favorite. I took a bite of the waffle and it tasted so sweet. But Adela wasn't eating. I grabbed her fork and knife and cut the pie and shoved it into her mouth. She scowled for a second and giggled as she swallowed the pie.

I smiled. "There, why aren't you eating your favorite pie? Did you lose your hands or something? Or maybe you lost your mouth eh?"

Adela laughed and her laugh got louder and louder. I started laughing, too. But when Charles smiled at Adela, Adela's laugh vanished and she kept on eating like it never happened.

I met his glance, but I sooner stared at my plate and continued eating. I wondered how it was going to be like in their fighting lessons. Maybe she can't help forgiving him in lessons. Or maybe she'll stay silent during lessons.

"Today is archery, right?" I asked carefully. "Shall I stay nearby during lessons?"

Adela shook her head and smiled softly. "No thanks. I am kind of sick right now. I am thinking of skipping class for today. I need to take a rest."

I was a little shocked to hear an unexpected answer. I looked at Charles, who seemed shocked as well. But Charles couldn't say anything to her. He nodded and tried to smile at her.

"All right," Charles said as he finished his breakfast. "As you wish, we'll take a rest just for today, but I hope you get better tomorrow and take lessons."

Charles gently tapped his lips with the tissue and stood up from where he was sitting. Then he smiled Adela again and left the room.

The awkwardness filled the air. I couldn't say anything but finish my waffle.

Adela stood up as well and looked at the queen and the king. She smiled politely and said, "Please excuse me." Then she got out of the room swiftly and shut the door.

Queen Georgina seemed confused and surprised. She turned to me and asked.

"What's all this mess? Mr. Henderson, is there something wrong between Charles and Adela?"

I swallowed and hesitated for a second.

"Uh, well I am not really sure, your highness. Maybe they had a small argument I guess, but I beg you not to worry about them. I am pretty sure that it'll be okay tomorrow."

King Jones, sitting next to the queen, seemed unconvinced. But he sooner squinted his eyes at me and shrugged.

"Kids," He said as he drank water from his glass. "They always fight, don't they?"

Queen Georgina seemed worried. "But they both looked a little upset.

Should I send the maids to help them solve the problem? Or should I meddle in their conflict?"

"No worries," I said. "It'll be fine. I know Adela perfectly. She'll forget what she was angry about tomorrow. She always does. So you don't have to worry about all this your highness. It is just a small fight."

The queen sighed and asked for a cup of tea to the maids. She stood up and so did the king.

"I hope everything gets solved all right." She said and left the room.

I sighed and turned around. There was Cathy, looking at me blankly.

"Why didn't you tell her what happened Lowell?" She yelled.

My face contorted. "Of course I shouldn't tell them you fool. This is just a small fight. I am pretty sure that they will be back to normal tomorrow. There's no need for the queen and the king to care about them."

Cathy thought about what I just told her. Finally she nodded and smiled.

"I guess you're right." Cathy said and stood up from her seat.

We left the dining room and walked upstairs toward Adela's room.

"Adela?" I knocked on the door. "Are you there?"

There was no reply from the other side of the door. I sighed and shrugged at Cathy. "Is she ever going to reply back?"

Cathy jumped up and down and knocked on the door as fast as she could.

"Come on Adela, can you please open the door? We know you are there. If you..."

The door creaked and Adela poked out the door. She was wearing her pajamas and had a blanket around her body to keep herself warm.

"Whoa," Cathy mumbled as she saw Adela in such a mess. "You are really sick!"

"Yeah of course I am. Did you think I lied to Lowell?"

She looked directly into my eyes and smiled. Her smile looked so sweet and warm. I could feel my eyes tremble. Gosh, I always can't control myself when she does that to me. It makes my heart beat so loudly.

"Come on in," Adela said. "I will make you a cup of tea."

Adela headed to the kitchen as we sat around her tea table beside her bed. The bed was all messed up as if it was telling me that Adela was lying there for the whole time.

"I am sorry. My room is quite a mess," She said as she put the pot on the stove. "I was lying in my bed right after I arrived in my room. I think I have flu. I thought it was just a cold, but it is worse than just a cold. Hey, feel my forehead."

She suddenly moved over to me. She stretched out her neck and grabbed my hand. She put it directly on her forehead and stared into my eyes again. It made me tremble.

"How is it?" She asked.

"Umm," I tried to control my heart beat, but couldn't. "It's burning hot."

"Yes it is." She said and moved over to the kitchen. She turned on the stove and sat with us.

"I think it's been a long time having teatime with you guys like this," Adela said happily. "You guys can come over as many times as you want."

Suddenly, the letters came into my mind. I rolled my eyes to search for the letters. I looked beside the bed, on the table, on the closet, but there were no letters caught on my eyes.

Adela felt this strange. "Lowell," She called and tried to follow my gaze. "Are you looking for something?"

"Huh?" I jumped and looked back at Adela. "No, I was just...well... nice room you got Adela. It is 2 times bigger than mine.

Adela laughed loudly and turned her head to check if the water's boiling. Then she turned back at us and shrugged.

"Well what did you expect? It's a princess's room."

"Oh, the water's boiling I think."

Adela ran to the kitchen and turned off the stove. Then she took out the cups and poured the hot water and petals of flower.

"There you go," She delivered the tea and sat down. The smell of sweet flower tickled my nostrils. I took and sip. It tasted just so sweet.

"So...anything fun going on?" She asked.

What are the letters about? Can I read them? I kept my questions inside and shut my mouth.

Cathy took a sip and smiled. "Well, we are here to ask you. How's everything going on these days Adela?"

"Oh, I almost forgot. Would you like some cinnamon cookies? They are quite delicious,"

We both nodded. Adela went back to the kitchen and brought a huge bowl filled with lots of cookies. The sweet scent of cinnamon filled the air.

"I tried baking it in this morning since I felt a little hungry and bored all by myself," She giggled. "I tried to recall the recipe that Brianna told me when I was young, but I am not sure I put the ingredients right."

I took a bite of a cookie. It tasted so sweet and the smell of cinnamon was harmonized with the savory taste of cookies. It tasted just like what Brianna made for us when were back in Anastelon. Aww, I already miss being in high school. I wished we could finish the quest quick and get back to our country and return to our own normal lives.

"Aww," Cathy smiled as she put the whole cookie into her mouth.

"I already miss Anastelon. It's been weeks since we left for this quest."

"Yeah it is quiet tiring," Adela sighed. "And a bit annoying sometimes. To be honest, I really don't like it here. I would love to get back to..."

"Devina right?" I interrupted as I munched on the cookies. Cracking sounds filled the air. Adela seemed a little surprised, but replied calmly. "No, I was going to say... Anastelon."

"Liar," Cathy snorted and grabbed another cookie. "Lowell is right. You are annoyed because you are mad that Charles hid the letters away from you, and you cried overnight obviously. This concludes that you have a crush on Jeffrey."

I coughed with shock. My heart pounded so fast. Inside of me was calling out to Adela, 'Don't say yes please. Tell her that it's not true.'

Adela stayed frozen and said nothing for a few minutes. Finally, she opened her mouth.

"No, I don't have a crush on him! I mean, we only met each other for just a short period. That doesn't make sense. And I didn't cry overnight. I told you in the dining room that I couldn't sleep because of the nightmare."

Cathy stared at her eyes for a long time like she didn't believe what she said.

"Okay well…to be honest, I am not sure about how I feel about him."

'Oh no, please change your words, Adela.' I begged inside.

"There you go, so you are going to go for him?" Cathy said excitedly.

"No, I am not sure. I…uh…I think I need to show you the letters he sent to me. That would be faster."

I shivered in agony. No Adela, you are thinking it wrong. You don't like him. You know you don't. I wanted to shout my words to her, but I kept my mouth shut.

She brought dozens of letters to our table and spread them all over the table. I carefully picked one of them with my shivering hands and started to read it off quickly.

Dear Adela
I know this is stupid but well…I thought it may be better to write to you so I can feel better. I beg you please don't throw

this away. It took me a big courage to write to you.

I am not sure if you changed your mind about this, but I just want you to know that I still think about you, every day, every night and every second. I was shocked to hear that you just wanted to stay as friends, and I tried hard to forget about you, but I realized I couldn't. You were my first lady and my first love. It is the first time to think...

I put the letter down and grabbed another one.

Dear Adela

Please...it's been weeks waiting for your reply. I know you are reading this. The mailman told me that the letters were delivered safely to Elsmiere. Then why aren't you writing back to me? All day and all night I can't stop thinking about you...

I grabbed another one. The three words caught my eye.

I ~~love~~ miss you

"This guy is total nonsense!" I shouted with anger. I stood up and threw the letters to the floor. Cathy and Adela stared at me blankly in horror. I couldn't bear it; I just couldn't stand this anymore. But soon, I calmed myself down and picked up the letters.

"I am sorry," I apologized to Adela. "I was just...angry because in boys' point of view, it seems like this guy is a total jerk..."

"He is not a jerk though..."

"I know. I know how you feel Adela. You are feeling sorry for him because you can't accept him. But when I see how he acts and how he writes to you, it feels like reading a fan letter. This guy is overly obsessed with you. And I am not blaming any one of you. I am just worried...about you."

"Worried about me?" She snorted. "But, why?"

"Because," I sighed. "You are my best friend and I have seen so many boys like this and most of them were jerks. Also, if you accept him as your boyfriend, it's going to be a huge issue around Anastelon. You can't risk that, can you?"

"Well, I have a different opinion," Cathy interrupted. "Adela, this Jeff guy is so sweet. Even I can feel his passion from these letters. He likes you, and you don't hate him, so why don't you go for him? I think he is quite nice."

"But, this guy is just a normal country boy who knows nothing about love," I shouted. "He will have Adela heartbroken."

"Well, you are talking way too aggressively. You should think about Adela's feelings."

"No, Cathy. It's fine. I don't feel anything at all." Adela stood up and took away the empty bowl and put it in the sink. She came back and sat down on her seat. "I understand both sides, and I think both of you are quite right. It'll take time for me to think about what I should do. First, maybe I should get the permission to write back to Jeff because I can't leave him like that. I will exchange letters for few times and see how I react. But it's still going to be a hard decision since my father and mother are probably going to reject him because he isn't a royal."

I nodded and so did Cathy.

"Okay, that seems like a good plan," I stood up. "I think we should go, right Cathy?"

Cathy stood up from her seat and hugged Adela. "Aww, I hope everything goes well with you, Adela."

"Yeah I hope so too." She murmured as she wrapped her arms around Cathy.

Adela looked at me and reached out her arm. "Come on Lowell."

I joined the group hug. I always loved the smell of Adela's hair. It smelled like strawberry and flowers. Her silky hair touched my mouth. I wrapped my arms around them and we stayed like that for a long time.

Heart Pounding

"I am surprised." Cathy said as she walked down the hallway. I looked at her with my contorted face.

"What makes you so surprised?"

"I thought you would agree with me," She said. "You know…letting her go out with Jeff. And do guys really see a boy like Jeff as a jerk? I think he's quite nice and romantic."

"Romantic?" I snorted. "I think you don't know anything about boys."

Cathy sighed. "Maybe you're right. I haven't gone out with any boys since birth, so how would I know? I mean, who would like me? I am fat, ugly, stupid…"

"No Cathy, ugh I am so sorry for saying that. I didn't mean it at all. I swear." I tried to cover up what I said, but Cathy didn't seem to believe me.

"Don't worry. I know myself. It's true that I don't know anything about boys because boys hate me." She stopped in front of her door. I stopped and looked into her eyes.

"Cathy," I said with my deep voice. "I am sure someday, you will meet a perfect guy. It's just that, it takes a little time to find that guy. Just wait and see."

Cathy's eyes twinkled. I'd never noticed that her eyes were so beautiful. We stared like that for a long time.

"Well, I don't know. Maybe the perfect guy can be a guy like you right?" Cathy said with hope.

My heart pounded with shock. I hesitated for a minute. "Wh…what do you mean? I'm not perfect."

"You are, Lowell," She smiled and unlocked her door. "You are."

She opened the door and slipped inside. "G'night." She said and closed the door.

What the heck is she talking about? I didn't get what she said, but I was somehow sure that it was a good meaning.

I shrugged and went along the hallway, to my room.

The telephone rang. I closed the book and picked it up.

"Hello?"

"Hey," A smooth voice came out from the phone. It was Adela. "Lowell, what are you up to?"

"Well, reading I guess. What's up?"

"I was going to go to gym and play basketball. Want to join me?"

"Sure," I stood up and grabbed my jackets from the chair. "I'll be at your door in a minute."

"Whoa," She giggled. "Slow down. I need to get changed into my PE clothes. We'll meet in 5 minutes. Okay?"

"Sure, see you then." I hung up excitedly and rushed to the bathroom. I looked myself in the mirror and checked my face and outfits. The clothes seemed a little untidy and wrinkled. But longer I looked, the more it looked cool. I tried combing my hair in many directions, but it became a mess at the end. So I had to comb it again and again until it seemed as usual.

I quickly ran out the room and to Adela's door. Adela was already waiting for me in front of her door. She looked so gorgeous as usual, with her long silky hair tied up in a ponytail and wearing velvet training suit. I always lose my words when I stand next to her.

"Hey Lowell," She called me and wrapped her arms around mine. "Why did it take so long?"

"Sorry, I had to finish the last line of 'The Sorrows of Young Werther'."

Adela's eyes popped out with surprise. "Oh my god, you are reading that book too? That book is my favorite! I highly recommend you to read it until the end."

I smirked. "Actually I've already read the book a long time ago. I was just skimming through the book swiftly. I found this book on the shelf in my room. There are a few of interesting books on the shelves."

"Oh, really? Maybe Charles put some books in your room as he knows you are a bookworm. That's awesome." She said and giggled.

"Well, it's too bad that I had read most of them before." I shrugged and said.

Adela's mouth made a shape of an 'o'. "Wow, is that true? You are so smart Lowell. I am so jealous of you."

"Nah, you can't say that I'm smart just because I read lots of books," I exclaimed. "You read lots of books too don't you?"

"Yeah but you always get the highest grades," She sighed. "You never get any Bs. You always get A plus, and you are known as the smartest kid in school…"

I didn't say anything as she lists some things that she thought I was good at. I just listened.

"…you get lots of prizes and…"

We finally got to the gym. The gym looked so huge, but it was smaller than Anastelon's. The gym was hollow unlike what I expected. Also, there were no coaches.

"Hmm, that's strange. In Anastelon, we had lots of people in the gym."

"Maybe Elsmiere doesn't allow citizens to use the gym," I said. "Come on, where's the ball?"

"Over there, beside the poll."

I swished to the poll and picked up the basketball. Then I dribbled it using my both hands."

"Come on Adel. Let me see your groovy tactics, huh?" I said and played with the ball as I bounced it on the ground.

Adela ran in and tried to take the ball away from me. But well, I knew she wouldn't win over the St. Lukes high basketball player.

About thirty minutes passed. I felt like my energy, perking up from the dead.

"Oh my god, I'm no match for you." Adela panted continuously as she collapsed on the floor. She kept breathing in and out and calmed her breath down, feeling tired, but I kept on dribbling around the gym until she got up.

"I think you are getting lazier. Maybe I should train you so you can get healthier. You can't lack your energy while on quest. You need some exercise."

Adela gasped in horror and moaned. "No," She groaned in pain. "This is too tiring. I think I need rest rather than exercise. Resting saves energy."

"Well," I chuckled and tapped her shoulder. "Come on, get up. You can't just lie down there for a whole day. You weren't like this when you were in Anastelon."

Adela grumbled and stood up slowly as if she had heavy rocks tied up on her bodies. She stood up and glared at me

"Don't say like that! Give me a break. I have flu, don't you remember?"

"Well, sorry I didn't remember that, but in fact, I do know that you don't have flu."

Adela's mouth made a shape of an 'o'.

"Lowell, you are being rude to me." She said with anger.

"Adela, admit it. You weren't sick at all from the first time. I've known you for years. You can't fool me with this stupid lie."

Adela sighed. "Ugh, fine. I am just a little sick. I feel a little queasy…"

I stared at her like I didn't believe what she said. Then she sighed again.

"Okay, I am completely healthy. I guess I am a little stressed out from all these heavy schedules."

"You are lying again Adela."

Adela stood frozen. "No I'm not."

"Come on, to be straightforward, you are not attending Charles' lessons because he hid the letters." I said loudly. Adela hesitated for a minute and didn't say anything. I really wanted to ask her how she is feeling about Charles and Jeffrey, but I decided to wait until she says something."

Minutes passed and she still had her mouth shut. She seemed as she was daydreaming. Maybe she is thinking about Jeffrey, I thought as I stood the heartaches from deep inside me. As I looked at her, I felt as if I was going to cry. Well, this is kind of stupid, but I was very desperate. I couldn't wait any longer. I had to spit it out or I was going to die by heart attack.

"Adela," I swallowed. I felt a huge lump inside my throat. "You and I are best friends right?" I decided to start off with simple questions, so that I can persuade her.

"Yes of course. Why are you asking that?"

"If we two are best friends," I said slowly. "We share everything together right?"

"Ugh, sure maybe."

"Then please would you be honest to tell me how you feel about Jeffrey and Charles to me right now?"

Adela hesitated and looked down. She stood like that for a long time and looked up at me. "Can you keep the secret?"

I nodded right away. "Of course, go on. I swear I won't tell anyone, even Cathy."

"Okay," She sighed and looked around for a place to sit. Then she walked toward the bench in the border of the gym. I followed her and we both sat down.

"I am being really honest with you Lowell. Since I don't have Brianna next to me, I need to tell you how I feel. Please don't be angry or mad at me after you hear this. Well, I read those letters from Jeffrey really carefully. I read them twice...no...I think I read them for like hundreds of times. They made me cry and smile and...actually, I read them right before I called you out to the gym. Before I called you out, I was crying in my room reading them over. The letters were full of sincerity. Then I thought if I was falling for him. I was frightened and confused so I threw the letters away and decided to call you out to the gym to turn my mind..."

Oh no, you shouldn't fall for him Adela, please...I begged inside desperately.

"So, you are...falling for him?" I asked carefully, wishing she would say no.

"Well, I still don't know. I am not sure. But the more I read the letters, I go red and miss him so much. It feels like, something weird down there is tingling up. Do you think that kind of feeling is love?"

My body was hardened like a rock. Oh no, Adela no. I had to stop her.

"No, definitely not," I said promptly. "Without a doubt, that is not the feeling of love. That...uh...that is...um...I bet that feeling is just an upsurge of sympathy, that's all. Loving someone is not that easy, especially for you Adela. You have never fallen in love in your whole life right?"

"Uh, yeah I guess."

"Yeah, that proves it. You met this guy for such a short period. You can't fall in love with him by those stupid...no sorry, I mean you can't be moved just by reading these letters. You are strong-minded about love, aren't you?"

"But, I can't stop thinking about him these days," She said unsurely. "So you're saying that it's all because I feel sad and sorry for Jeffrey?"

I swallowed and calmed my heart down from aching. "Of course, believe me. I totally understand how you feel. I've experienced that kind of feeling for lots of times. It happens to many people frequently."

Adela sighed. "Argh, I just want to talk to him really. I want to say sorry for leaving him behind and...sorry for not accepting him."

"Nah, you shouldn't worry about that one bit," I patted her shoulders gently and stood up. "I know guys. They forget about things easily, even love."

Adela stood up as well. "Are you sure about that Lowell?"

"Of course," I said without thinking. "Come on, one more game. All right?"

Adela smiled and snatched the ball. "Okay, let's go."

I ran down the stairs. My heart kept on beating and beating as my steps got faster. I ran down the hall swiftly and looked for anyone. Then I found a servant walking down the hall carrying a huge box of laundries.

I grasped his shoulder tightly as I stopped running. The servant dropped the laundry box with his face in surprise.

"Oh my god," The servant yelled in shock. "You scared me to death, sir. What's wrong?"

I panted for minutes, and then I choked out the words.

"I…need…your…help…it's an emergency." I panted hard as I said to him. I could feel my mouth getting dry from breathing too hard.

"What happened?" The servant asked worriedly.

I had to stop it, and I knew how to stop it.

Adela

"Do you think that
kind of feeling is love?"

Soaked up with Tears

Dear Adela

I woke up this morning and opened the windows as usual. I saw the sun shining brightly and wondered if you were staring at it too. Starting off days by thinking of you is becoming a part of my life, and sometimes I feel my heart beating so fast, and sometimes my heart aches so bad. My heart is yearning for you Adela...I feel it deep inside me.

I hope you think of me. I hope you think of me as the way I think of you. But well, I guess it doesn't work out that way for you. I tried to understand you every day and every moment whenever my heart starts beating for you. But I realized I couldn't. You are too amazing for me. It feels like you are controlling over me. I know this looks so weird and lame, but my whole body feels that way.

Grandpa Louis always tells me, "She's gone. You are an idiot. You will never meet her again." But Grandma tells me, "I totally understand how you feel, tell Adela everything and how you feel about her. Then she'll come back whatever happens." I don't know who to believe, but I want to believe that grandma is right. These letters I am sending you are the last hope. I need you so bad.

I miss you so much Adela...Why wouldn't you write back to me? It doesn't matter. I will write to you until you write me back. Please tell me how you feel...please...for me...

Jeff

I touched my swollen red eyes with my fingers. I realized, my eyes were burning hot. I have never cried for such a long time like this for someone who loves me. It made me feel awful.

I couldn't stand this any longer. I had to write to him. It would be mean not to write him back. He wants a reply so bad… I can't wait and see like this.

I thought it would make me feel better when I write to him back and tell him that I read all of his letters, and understand him completely.

But I soon realized that Charles was never going to let me write back to him. "You should concentrate in this quest! It costs your neck!" I could almost hear his ringing voice in my head. I made a funny face as I thought of Charles. Ugh, I am starting to hate him, I thought.

Anyway, I had to write back to him whatever happens. But where should I go? What should I do first? I thought and stood up. I loitered around the room as I thought of the plan. Maybe I should ask the maid… no…that could leak into Charles' ears. Maybe I should get Cathy or Lowell to help me out with it. Well, Cathy…she understands me totally and she doesn't think of Jeff in a bad way. But I sooner recalled that she is not that secretive. She'll end up telling what I did in front of everyone. That is too dangerous.

Hmm, what about Lowell? He doesn't tell secrets to other people. That makes me feel safe and reliable. But he said that Jeff is idiotic. Maybe he may hate helping Jeff. But he was a better option in this situation. I ran to the phone and pressed Lowell's room number.

I nervously held onto the phone and waited as I heard the signal went. I waited and waited, but there was no answer. I put the phone down. It's strange. He couldn't be out right after exercising. Maybe he's taking a shower and couldn't answer his phone, I thought.

The clock was pointing 4:15pm and I had to figure out how to rewrite Jeff before dinner. The dinner was 6 and I had less than two hours. I had to move quickly.

I should go to the post office. I sprinted out the room and closed the door.

I tiptoed slowly across the hallway toward the gate. Just a few more steps, I was out for freedom. Isn't this thrilling?

"What are you doing there?" A familiar voice caught me frozen. I slowly looked around and saw Charles looking at me doubtfully. I just stood there, looking at him for a long time. My heart started to pound so fast.

"What…what are you doing here?" I asked, trembling in shock.

"Well, I was about to attend the family meeting. What about you Adela? You are not going outside right?"

"Erm, actually, I was about to go out."

Charles squinted his eyes full of suspicion. "Why are you going out?"

"Um, because…well I decided to take some fresh air. I feel so squeezed."

"Oh, really? But don't you have to call the security with you?"

As he finished the word, two men from the security came aside me. They were well-dressed with same suits and same sunglasses. They vowed to me and said, "Your highness, we will take care of you on your way."

I hesitated and looked at Charles. "I don't need two. One is enough I think. I will be back as soon as possible."

"May I ask where you're going?"

I trembled and quickly thought of an excuse.

"Uh, I just wanted to…you know…look around Elsmiere. I see it's a nice weather out there. I can't miss this day."

"All right. I will tell my mother where you'll be. You should take two guys with you. It is unsafe to be on your own."

"I know, but I just need one guard with me. I will be back in an hour, I promise." I kept on insisting.

Charles gave up. "All right. You can choose who you'll take. I will go tell my mother. But be sure to get back before dinner."

"Okay thank you so much." I sighed in relief and rolled my eyes at two guards standing stiff in front of me.

"All right," I sighed and stared at their figures. I had to take the smaller one so I can deal with the guard easily.

I noticed that the left guy was about 3 inch taller than the right guy. I looked at the right guy and asked. "What's your name?"

"It's Giles, ma'am." He vowed and replied politely.

"Giles," I pushed the gate open and said. "Come along with me please?"

We walked outside and closed the gate behind us. I could see many people walking by and it was somehow different from Anastelon. I awkwardly stepped forward. Giles came aside me and tried to surround me with his long arms. As he did that, suddenly everyone stared at us curiously. I tapped on Giles' wide back.

"Hey Giles, please don't overreact. Can't we just walk normal? I mean, all those people are staring at us because you are surrounding me like that."

Giles turned his head to me. "No ma'am, they are staring at us because we just came out of the castle. My job is to take care of you, so this is appropriate for both of us."

"Okay, fine. I am going to the post office. Can you take me there?"

Giles shrugged. "Well, the post office is too far away, you should take the carriage to get there miss. Shall I call the carriage?"

"Yes, please."

Giles quickly took out the walkie-talkie from his pocket and turned it on.

The walkie-talkie made a buzz sound. He pressed on the red button and started talking.

"Answer me hippo," He said as he puts the walkie-talkie close to his mouth.

A few seconds later, the walkie-talkie buzzed again. "Hippo's here. Who's on?'

"It's tiger. Princess Monette from Anastelon is now hoping to go to the post office. Come by the gate ASAP. Got it?"

The walkie-talkie buzzed again. "Got it, tiger." It said.

I stared at Giles confusedly. Giles looked at me and let out a loud laugh. "Ha ha ha, I know it may make you confused miss. They are secret nicknames for people who work here in the palace. Mine's tiger and the hippo, which I just said, is the one who's going to bring the carriage. Oh, there he comes!"

I looked around. There was a small carriage with two white lovely horses and a short man was sitting in the front, holding the reins to control the horses. I kept watching it as it came along. The short man pulled the reins and the horses let out a cry and stopped.

"Your highness," The short man vowed and smiled. "I would be very honored to take you to the post office." I got on the carriage and Giles got on it after me. He closed the carriage door behind and the carriage started to move forward.

Everyone stared at the carriage that I was in. I looked out and could see many small buildings with flowers. Sellers were selling flowers, flower juice, veggies, flower seeds, and many other things. The houses were mostly filled with flowers and plants.

"Wow, there are so many flowers in this place!" I exclaimed.

"Yes," Giles opened his mouth. "Elsmiere is an eco-friendly country. It is law that in Elsmiere all houses should have at least 2 flowers each. But even without that law, people living in Elsmiere love flowers so much that there are no people breaking that law."

"That's amazing."

"And, because there are many flowers, there are many bees. Honey is our specialty. We have the best honey in the whole world. I recommend buying some before you leave Elsmiere, miss."

"Yes, that would be wonderful. Thank you for the recommendation."

I said as I gazed at millions and millions of flowers.

"What kind of flowers do people of Elsmiere mostly prefer?" I asked.

Giles thought for a moment. "Well, I heard they prefer sunflowers. Sunflowers can be used in many ways. Their buds, petals, and seeds are edible."

"Oh," I nodded my head. "I see. Elsmiere is such a nice country except for the people who has pollen allergy."

We laughed as the carriage rolled along the rocky road. 5 minutes passed and we finally arrived in front of the post office. I got off the carriage and so did Giles.

"I will wait here until Princess Monette comes back." The short man said loudly.

I had to make Giles stay back when I write a reply to Jeffrey. I had to do something before I go inside the post office.

"Hey, Giles," I said in a friendly tone. "Can you buy some ice creams from that shop over there?"

Giles turned around and checked the shop. "Yes of course ma'am."

I waved at him. "Then I will be in the post office when you buy some ice cream from that shop so we can save time. Okay?"

"But my duty is to take care of you right beside you, your highness." He said without moving.

I started begging. "Come on, we are out of time. We need to get back to the castle quickly. Please do as what I say for just this time."

Giles sighed. "All right miss, I'll do as you say. What flavor?"

"Chocolate," I said quickly. "And after you buy some ice cream, please buy some more foods from other stores, that you recommend me to eat. Can you do that for me too?"

"Sure, I will be right back."

Giles went to the ice cream shop while I went inside the post office. I had to write a letter to Jeffrey as quick as I could before Giles comes. I bought a letter and borrowed a pen from the counter and started writing.

Dear Jeffrey

I am really sorry I didn't write back to your letters. I got your letters this week and read them all yesterday. Most of them made me cry, and I could feel your passion and love from all your letters. I know you are desperate to have me as your girlfriend, but for me it is a serious part that I need to think about carefully. Also, right now I think I still want to be just friends with you. But I am starting to feel that my heart is moving. I asked Lowell if this feeling was love, but he said that it isn't. I guess he's right. I think you should wait and see what happens to me. Maybe my mind can possibly change while we exchange letters. So don't be so depressed.

I looked around and checked if Giles was near. My hand was trembling and my forehead was all sweaty. I quickly continued the words.

Charles doesn't like me reading letters from you. I am not sure why, but I think it's because I should concentrate on my work in Elsmiere. I have such busy schedules in here. I train everyday with Charles. So I hope you understand if I send back letters late.
I hope I could meet you again after this quest. Please write me back. I will write back soon as I can this time.
Adela

I scrawled my words as quickly as I could and put it in the envelope. I wrote the address that I remembered from Jeffrey's envelope covers. I held the envelope with my trembling hands and waited in the queue to give the envelope to the counter, so that they could send this letter to Jeffrey.

I could feel my heart pounding. I kept looking around to check if Giles was back from shopping. Fortunately, there was no sign of him.

At last I gave the envelope to the counter and rushed outside. I could see Giles still shopping in a shop across the street. He was holding a tower of boxes of goods that he bought. I gasped and ran to him.

"Oh my goodness, you bought a lot, Giles!"

Giles turned around. "Oh, your highness, you are back," I could see the boxes wobble in the air. "I was about to leave the shop. Did I buy too much? Well, I don't think it's too much. There are still hundreds of specialties left. If you want some more of them, I can get…"

"No these would be enough." I helped him carry those boxes. We both carried the boxes into the carriage and the carriage started heading back to the castle.

"Where's Olivia?" I asked Charles. We were heading back to our rooms after dinner. The dinner was great. They gave us ravioli with savory cream sauce and chocolate mousse for dessert. It was so good that I almost ate the whole plate.

Charles hesitated for a second. "Oh, Olivia…didn't you know that she is gone to study abroad? It has been a long time and you didn't realize that she was gone?"

I gasped. "What do you mean? She couldn't be gone that fast! Why is she studying abroad? Where did she go? When will she come back?"

"Whoa geez," He chuckled a little. "Well, she is just gone for about a month. The she'll come back. I am not sure about where she is right now. There are some things that I can't tell you Adela."

I stared at Charles' face. He tried to grin, but his face was hardened. Charles was acting strange. It was a fake smile, I realized.

"All right. I will see you tomorrow. Hope you get better. I will see you in the morning then."

"Okay." I said as I opened my room's door with my key. I unlocked the door and turned my head to Charles. I waved him good bye.

Boxes of goods that Giles bought for me were standing beside the door. I opened one of them and took out a bag of crackers. It said, 'Honey Belly' on the cover.

I changed my formal clothes into comfortable clothes and jumped into my bed. I should go to bed early, I thought and opened the cracker bag. I grabbed a handful of crackers and put them in my mouth. They tasted sweet like honey.

"What should I do now...?" I said to myself as I looked around the room. Then my eyes caught a book that Lowell gave me. I grabbed the book and started to read the first line of very first page.

'The Silence of the Darks

Has the information of forbidden history of Vulgary and its related countries.'

That grasped my interest. What would be the secret of Vulgary? Does anyone know about these secrets? What is this book?

I kept wondering as I scanned through the pages. I quickly looked through the pictures first. There were pictures of scary monsters from Vulgary clans. There were pictures of dead corpses. That gave me chills on my back and made me imagine if I could fight over them with my skills that I learned from Charles. As I was thinking on my own, I kept looking for pictures. Then suddenly, I froze as I turned on the next page. My heart stopped and I couldn't breathe for a minute.

There was a medium-sized picture in the corner of the page. It showed a man getting his neck cut off by the woman from the Vulgary clan. The woman from the Vulgary clan looked so familiar. So familiar that I could notice who it was at once.

The woman in the picture was Ms. Kimberly from math class.

The Truth

I rushed over to the telephone and called Lowell. This time, Lowell answered.

"Hello?" He said with his faint voice.

"Lowell!" I said as I freaked out. "The...there is Ms. Kimberly!"

Lowell sounded confused. "Pardon? Did you just say Ms. Kimberly?"

"Yes!" I shrieked. I carefully checked the photo for many times, but it was the exact same as Ms. Kimberly.

"Who's Ms. Kimberly? Oh, wait. I think I've heard of her..."

"Yeah, she is our math teacher. Don't you know?"

"Oh, you mean that teacher that we talked about in cafeteria?" He asked.

"Yes, Lowell. I think it'll be better to come over to my room right now with Cathy. I think Cathy should know this too."

"All right. I will go to your room with Cathy." We hung up. About few minutes later, the doorbell rang and I opened the door. Cathy and Lowell were standing in front of the door.

I let them in.

"Please show me the picture that you found." Lowell hastened. I handed the picture to them with my shaking hands.

"Oh my god," Cathy screamed in shock. "What is Ms. Kimberly doing over here? What is this book?"

"Oh, it's a book that Lowell stole for me from the library," I told her. "Lowell, I thought you recommended me this book because you saw this picture."

Lowell's eyes got bigger and shook his head.

"No, I haven't read this book before. I just read the very first page and thought that it may be helpful for you, Adela. That's why I gave you this book. Also, I hadn't taken her class, remember?"

We all stared at the photo for a long time. It was exactly the same as Ms. Kimberly. Her long black hair and tanned skin matched with what I saw, except in the picture the woman had darker eyes than Ms. Kimberly.

Suddenly, Lowell's fingers pointed at the caption below the picture. He said, "Look at this."

We all read the caption.

Soldier No. 564 Vincent Marcus met a glorious death at the battle by Katrina Vulgary from Vulgary clan.

"This is not Ms. Kimberly!" I exclaimed in confusion. "It says that this woman is Katrina."

"But she looks exactly the same as Ms. Kimberly! How can this happen?" Cathy yelled.

Lowell thought for a second. "There are many people who look alike. And you can't trust pictures completely. You have to check the real person to see if it's really her." Lowell said.

"Maybe she is Ms. Kimberly's twin sister," Cathy said thoughtfully. "Or maybe Ms. Kimberly could be one of the Vulgary clan and she is acting like human in front of us."

"I remember her eye color. They were light brown." I said.

"Well, what color are Vulgarians' eyes?" Cathy asked.

"Their eyes are completely black, so black that you can't see their pupils. You know, we can see each other's pupils because our irises are generally more light-colored than the pupils."

"Whoa, that would be a little spooky to look at."

"So to differentiate between Vulgarians and other people, you should see if their pupils are seeable. Also, you should check if there is a unique tattoo on the back of their neck. If someone has all these features, that person is definitely a Vulgarian." I explained to Cathy and Lowell. These facts were from what I read from those books when I was in Anastelon.

"I am confused right now." Cathy said as she grabbed her hair with her both hands.

"There is just one way to find out the truth," Lowell said seriously. "We can ask Charles about this."

"Charles?" I yelled in shock. "We stole his book. That's not going to happen, Lowell. He'll have us in jail."

"We can say that we heard a rumor that one of our teachers called Ms. Kimberly is one of the Vulgarians. Can't we?" Lowell said thoughtfully.

Cathy nodded and smiled. "I think that's quite a great idea."

I shrugged. "Well, I don't know. Charles may find out. He's not that foolish."

"Well, we can try just once," Cathy said. "If you're nervous, I will ask him for you."

"No thanks, maybe we shouldn't ask him about anything. He would be suspicious at us after he saw us stealing his keys."

"Yeah you're right," Lowell said and nodded. "All right. First, can I have some of your cookies Adela? I am hungry right now."

I giggled and rushed over to the piles of boxes. "Hey you know what? Take armful of these cookies. I have tons of them." I opened the box. Lowell and Cathy's eyes widened with surprise and joy.

"Oh my goodness, you are living in heaven!" Cathy screamed and jumped up and down. "You are such an angel, thank you so much Miss Monette."

Lowell stared at the clock on the wall. "I think I should go and take a shower."

Cathy glanced at it too. "Oh, so do I. Thank you so much for the cookies."

"It's okay, guys. If you need more, come over to my room and take some more. See you tomorrow."

I waved as they closed the door behind them. I walked over to the bed and grabbed the book. I stared at the picture again for a long time and tried to picture Ms. Kimberly on Vulgary clan. Her image fits perfectly with this character, I thought. But, that photo can't be her.

Or can it be?

More and more Training

- Triple swing-keep your legs spread out
- Double swing plus diagonal swing-speed is important
- Diagonal attack-speed
- Stabbing hard-strength
- Swing diagonally

I wrote some notes down of what I learned in Charles' class. For 2 months, everyday, for six hours, I learned using swords from him. At first it was so hard to learn how to use and grab the sword, but as I practiced every day with him, my moves started becoming natural. It made my heart pound and focus hard on the fight.

"All right, diagonal, that's good, spread your legs! Spread your legs! You're doing great. Stay focused on my sword." Charles yelled as we practiced sword fighting. I panted as I quickly swung my arms around with my sword. My sword made clinking sounds as it hit his sword. I slightly jumped forward and pushed against him with my sword. Charles looked disconcerted and started attacking wildly on me as he swung his sword. I didn't want to lose, this time. I put my whole power in my hands and pushed his sword downwards. His sword slipped out of his hands and fell onto the ground. We both stared at the fallen sword for a long time and looked at each other. Charles smiled and chuckled with joy.

"Oh my goodness," Charles clapped his hands. Then everyone else (servants and guards) around me started clapping at me. I laughed pleasurably and looked around. Where are Cathy and Lowell? Did they see me in this fight? This is incredible. I beat the prince of Elsmiere! I screamed inside.

I grinned at Charles and picked up the sword. "This is nothing. I can show you more next time. You should be careful Charles."

I laughed and walked away from him. A few servants gathered around me, offering towels and a bottle of water. I grabbed the towel and grabbed the water. I drank down the water as fast as I could and cooled down my throat. I panted and panted as my heart pounded as if it was going to explode.

"Yes!" I screamed in excitement as I walked across the field and to the door. "I finally beat Charles!"

I glanced at the bench where Lowell always used to sit. He was there, closing his book and looking at me with his sweet smile. I hugged him and jumped up and down.

"Oh my god, Lowell. I finally beat Charles! Can you believe it? It's the first time. I can't believe I'm this good."

Lowell chuckled as he hugged me back. "Whoa Adela, you did sweat a lot. You should really need to take a shower."

Lowell stood up and brought me to my room.

I took a shower. I sang my favorite songs in the shower; all those exciting songs that I can think of. I used to lose whenever I competed with Charles, but this time, I finally won. Well, maybe he let me win on purpose, but the feeling of victory felt so sweet more than a dip of honey. I got out of the steamy shower and got changed into fresh new clothes that just got in from laundry. My mind was as light as ever.

After I dried my hair, I grabbed my ribbon and stood in front of the mirror. There she was, the wonderful girl who won the prince of Elsmiere. She smiled as she tied her long curly hair into a ponytail. Then I smiled at her as I looked into her green enchanting eyes.

"Adela," I mumbled at myself. "Win again next time, will you?"

"Wow, I'd never tasted such good meat like this." I exclaimed as I wildly cut the thick steak with the knife. Everyone else in the dining room kept gazing at me as they ate like I was an animal in the zoo. Their looks seemed weird.

King Jones chuckled and took a sip from his glass. "Well, Adela," He opened his mouth first. "You seem very ecstatic today. Is there any good news you want to share with us?"

"Yes, actually, I finally won Charles for the first time I've been training." I said without any hesitance. "Isn't this great?"

"Ah," Queen Georgina smiled as she swallowed the chunk of meat. "Well, that's great Adela, congratulations. Oh, Charles we are holding a ball before they leave to Vulgary right? It's been a long time not holding any parties." She whispered to King Jones. King Jones nodded and finished his last bite. He wiped his lips gently with the handkerchief and stood up from his seat.

"Attention everyone," He said with his ringing loud voice. "I have an announcement to make. Today, our lovely Adela, princess of Anastelon won over our Prince Jones for the first time, which seems like a huge development. Well done Adel, and keep up the good work, my son,"

"Thank you very much, father." Charles and I both replied.

"And Adela. I should warn you. There are still many skills that you still have to learn,"

I choked on my water. I coughed and coughed and wanted to check if what I just heard was well-said.

I tapped my mouth with the cloth and cleared my throat. "I beg your pardon?"

"As I repeat what I just said, there are still several skills you have to achieve. For example, horse riding, driving chariots, and most importantly as I heard, Aians should know how to transform into animals. So later on when you learn quite many of the skills you will have to learn how to transform into animals from an expertise, not from Charles. As you may know, none of our family members are Aian, so you have to learn from someone who has Aian blood."

I couldn't get away from the shock. I thought the sword fights were the end of the skill. But there were still so many more skills that I had to learn.

My head started to ache. "Gosh, when am I going to learn all those things? It's going to take ages…"

"No, Adela," Charles interrupted. "I have all the plans. It is going to work out well in shorter time than you think. I promise."

I groaned and rolled my eyes. Charles looked into my eyes firmly as he was full of conviction. I sighed, nodding heavily.

"All right. Well…there's no way that I can get away with it. Screw it!"

Lowell clapped his hands. "I am so proud of you Adela. I will always stay beside you."

Cathy glared at Lowell nervously and clapped her hands too.

"So will I. We will always support you Adela, Lowell and me."

I smiled at them and felt so much energy coming from deep inside of me. It felt like it was getting bigger and bigger.

I can do this. I reached my first step. There's no reason I won't reach other steps, I thought.

Other Lessons

It was the next morning. Charles and I were standing in the middle of the grassy field, which we always do training as usual. It was a windy day and with no clouds in the sky.

"It's such a wonderful weather!" Charles exclaimed as his silky hair waved along the wind. "Perfect for horse riding."

I was confused. "Wait a minute, where are our swords and shields? Aren't we supposed to...?"

"Nope, today we will try something different. It's quite boring to practice just one for weeks. I should teach you horse riding today."

"Oh my god," I jumped up and down excitedly. "Actually I had tried horse riding once, actually it was a pony but anyway, I remember that it was so fun. Except it was so shaky it got me back pain after riding."

Charles laughed hard. "Well Adela, this time, horse riding isn't for fun. It's for fighting enemies, so you should concentrate and listen to what I say. All right?"

Charles called the servant from afar and made a signature with his hands. The servant nodded and opened the gate of the stable. The gate croaked and he went inside. About a minute later, my eyes were widened and my mouth made a shape of an 'o'.

There were two huge horses walking out of the gate. One of them was black and the other one was white. The black one looked so pretty and brave. It reminded me of the novel, Black Beauty by Anna Sewell. It was one of my favorite books.

"Wow." I mumbled and slowly reached out my hand to the black horse. It closed its eyes and craned over to my hand. When our skins met, the touch made me feel mesmerized.

"Charles," I turned to Charles and pleaded. "Can I have this beautiful horse? She is so…indescribably pretty."

"Of course, Adela," Charles smiled. "But how did you know that it was 'she'?"

I stroked the horse's neck as I admired the horse. I hesitated and finally opened my mouth.

"She has…such beautiful eyes."

"Your highness, may I?" The servant pulled the horses' reins as other couple of servants hurried over with metal stairs which are used to get on the horse. I slowly climbed the stairs and stood in front of the horse's back. I carefully sat on the horse and grabbed the reins. I could feel my muscle harden and I was stiff. It felt so amazing to ride such a pretty horse like this one.

The guy who looked like a horse trainer came across to me.

"Hello, princess," He bowed and said. "Please, would you slap your horse with the rope as lightly as you can?"

I took a deep breath and slapped the horse with the rope lightly as I could. The horse started walking. Oh my god, that felt so amazing. This beautiful thing was walking along the green field with me on its back. This felt awesome.

"If you want to speed up, you may slap it one more, but don't forget to slap it lightly or else this horse may run too fast, all right? And if you want to stop, pull the reins." The trainer shouted.

"I've got it!" I shouted back as I looked around the captivating views around the castle. Everything seemed so beautiful; colorful flowers, trees dancing in the cool breeze and behind them were the tall castle and a tower with a sharp peak. I couldn't shut my mouth. It was so magical.

"Hey, Adela," A voice called me from behind. I turned around.

Charles was on his horse and the horse was running fast toward me. His hair swished in the wind as always and his smile was so gorgeous. I'd never noticed him that handsome.

"You're really good." Charles said as he pulled his reins. The horse quickly stopped right next to my horse.

"Wow," I stared at him amazed. "How can you do that? Maybe I can go faster."

I slapped the rope a little harder and my horse started to speed up. A minute later we arrived in front of the gate where Lowell reads books. I searched for Lowell. He was reading his book on the bench as always.

"Hey Lowell," I shouted as loud as I could for him to hear me. "Look at me! I am on a horse! Isn't this amazing?"

Lowell lifted his head from his book and stared at me for a long time.

He shouted back, "Great job, Adela. You're good."

After horse riding for half an hour, I was acclimatized to being on a horse. It felt almost as natural as riding a horse for years. I could guarantee that I was born to ride a horse. It was my instinct.

"Wow, Adela. I am impressed," Charles came over with his horse. "You've got talent."

"Thanks." I pulled the rope and stopped. "Um, can I get down?"

"Sure." Charles jumped off his horse and ran toward me. He reaches out his arms and grabbed my waist. I put my hands on his shoulders and jumped off the horse. But I jumped off with too much strength that I fell on top of him.

"Ugh." Charles grunted as he fell on his back.

When I opened my eyes, we were facing so close, lying on the ground. His warm breath tickled my chin and his beautiful eyes stared right through mine. My face got hotter and hotter. For that moment I was frozen and my heart was beating so loudly that I was worried if he could hear my heart beat. But when I woke up from day dreaming, I jumped and stood up.

I didn't know what to say. "I...I am so sorry Charles...Are you all right?"

Charles stood up from the ground. "I...am fine." He looked absolutely absent-minded.

I could feel my face turning scarlet. "I've got to go. I'll see you later." I ran to the gate and passed where Lowell was sitting. Lowell spotted me and ran after me.

"Adela," Lowell yelled. "What were you doing with Charles just a minute ago? Were you guys…?"

"No, no, no nothing happened. It's just…I fell on top of him. That's all."

"Then why are you hiding away?" He asked hurriedly.

"Well, I am sorry Lowell. I don't feel like talking with you right now, so I will see you later. I've got to take a shower."

I ran across the hall and up the stairs. I rushed into my room and closed the door behind me.

What was that feeling about? I wondered. My heart was still rumbling inside me. I touched my boiling cheeks.

Why am I acting this way? It felt so different from how I felt with Lowell and Cathy…and even Jeffrey. The moment when I fell into his wide arms…I wished I could rewind back.

I got my breath back, but my heart was still burning and pounding crazily. So I took a quick shower and fell into my bed. I stared at the ceiling for a long time. On the ceiling, my eyes kept on drawing Charles' gorgeous smile. His dimple looked ever so lovely and his silky hair always flew in the wind. And his amazing eyes…He leaned over me and puckered I blinked my eyes for many times, but he was still there.

I got up from my bed and murmured.

"I am in love with him." I murmured blankly

Wake up, brush my teeth, eat breakfast, training, eat lunch, training, eat dinner, training until 10, rest, go to bed; these are my lists of daily life and I was so tired of it!

It felt okay at first, but day after day, these jammed schedules made me gain lots of stress.

"Just eat what you're given you silly old pig!"

"Come on, can't you go faster for heaven's sake?"

"I just hate my life."

Yup, everything, I mean everything was getting on my nerves, even when I wasn't on my period. I just hated everything I saw, touch, hear or feel. So everyone around me had to stay silent and careful. What a marshmallow. Such cowards.

I was walking down the hall to the post room where one of the maids told me to go when I look for Jeff's mail. I peeked inside and saw an old lady, dressed in a neat knitted sweater, writing with her pen on a notebook. She kept her eyes focused on the paper until I knocked on the door. She lifted her head and said with her croaky voice, "Oh, come in."

I carefully walked inside and stood in front of the counter. She smiled brightly at me and asked, "What's your full name?"

"It's Adela Beth Monette."

"Let me see..."She stood up from her seat and walked toward the shelves. In the shelves, there were hundreds of files and papers. She looked through the corner that said M on it and took out a file and flipped through the letters. She kept on searching for minutes, but she shook her head and closed the file.

"I am sorry. There are no letters for you dear." She turned to me and said.

My heart started to pound in nervousness. "That can't be!" I shouted. "Jeff would have sent me a letter by now. I sent my letter last week. It takes him just a couple of days to reply."

The lady flipped open the same file again and looked through the letters for the second time. After a minute, she closed the file and sighed. "No sweetie. I've checked twice, but there are no letters for you. Maybe you should come around the other time."

I sighed and turned around. What's happening with Jeff? He sent me so many letters before I sent a reply. But after I wrote back to him, he stopped writing me back. Isn't that strange?

I started to get worried. What if I sent my letter too late and he is angry at me? I bit my lips and headed to the back garden where training goes. Charles was feeding his horse with a handful of hay. The horse was eating fast as if it was going to swallow his whole hands.

I walked toward him with my droopy shoulders. Charles turned to me and smiled with his cute dimple. "Any luck?" He asked.

I shook my head and sighed. "Huh, it's been a week since I haven't received any letters. What's happening? It makes me so worried."

Charles shrugged and handed me some hay. "Here. Feed yours."

I grabbed the hay and held it out to my horse. "There you go, Beauty." I murmured as she munched on the hay. Charles looked at me with his eyes wide with surprise. "Beauty?" He said. "Is that her name?"

"Yeah," I nodded. "She reminds me of the novel called Black Beauty. I named her after that. Also, she looks so beautiful, doesn't she?"

"Well, not as beautiful as you, Adela."

I froze. I stared at him for a long time as he fed his horse as if nothing happened. I felt my cheeks burning and my legs shivered.

I decided to ignore his last words. "What's your horse's name?"

He looked back at me. "His name's Beast. I named him that for him to be strong and powerful, just like a beast."

Suddenly and idea popped inside my head. I clicked my fingers and jumped up and down excitedly.

"Oh my god, that's perfect! My horse can be the Beauty and your horse can be the Beast, and together they can be Beauty and a Beast!"

Charles chuckled. "What a wonderful idea! Let's go like that then."

Beauty coughed as she munched all of the hay. My hands were soaked with her saliva. I squeezed her reins and got on her back. She sniffed and let out a little cry as if she was excited to have me on her back.

Charles stared at me for a long time. I tried to avoid his eyes, but at last I had to stare back to make him feel embarrassed. But his eyes did not move away from mine. Our eyes kept on staring at each other. I squinted my eyes and asked, "Why...are you looking at me like that?"

He took a short breath and quickly moved his eyes away. "It's nothing,"

He mumbled. "Hey Adela, we are going to learn how to use arrows and bows today, but first since we are already on our Beauty and the Beast, maybe we can first enjoy the breeze for half an hour and then go for bow and arrow. Is that okay for you?"

I nodded and smiled. "Sure, that'd be okay."

I stared at the sky. Some muffy grey clouds were dominating the sky. The chills ran down my back as the cold wind blew through my clothes.

"Charles, don't you feel kind of cold?" I asked. "I think it's going to rain soon. Maybe we should stop this."

He shrugged. "Well, maybe we should stop this when it rains," He said. "Come on, let's go. I teach you bow and arrow."

Bow and arrow was quite difficult. At first he taught me how to grab the bow. It was quite uncomfortable, but I managed to do it soon. But the gloomy weather kept on bothering me. I kept looking up the sky that seemed that it would rain soon. But Charles ignored the weather.

"Come on Adela, don't be too distracted. You are not concentrating."

"I know, I know… But the weather…"

"Please stop complaining about the weather. It's not going to rain Adela."

But the raindrops started falling from the sky, drop by drop. I felt a raindrop land on my nose, but I decided to concentrate.

A few minutes later, the drops were countlessly falling from the overcast sky. And even worse, there were thunders roaring through the air. I stopped shooting arrows and looked at Charles.

"We should get inside. It's pouring!" I shouted, but Charles didn't seem to move an inch. He acted as if it was not raining at all. He looked sharply back at me and said, "Adela, it's not raining, so now stop complaining and keep practicing."

"What?" I yelled in despair. "It's not raining? Then what about this water coming from the sky, huh?"

Charles' face didn't even change a bit. "Nothing, so keep going. Come on. We are going inside when you hit the target, I promise."

Wow, this guy was going to pull me to death. My eyes were all blurred from all the pouring rain. I could not even see the target, which was about 30 meters away from me. It was impossible for me to hit the target in this horrible weather.

I dropped my bow and yelled to Charles. "I can't do this! It's my first time and it's pouring! How am I supposed to do this in this weather?"

Charles glared at me as if he was sick of my complaints.

"You can do it, Adela. Just try it."

Ugh, I sighed loudly and picked up my bow and an arrow. I pulled the string and tried to point at the mark. I let go of the arrow and it flew in the rain and then easily fell down on the ground.

I thumped my foot in anger and grabbed another arrow. It is Charles' fault, I thought as I pulled the string again and pointed the mark. The arrow flew across the yard and crashed onto the ground. I grunted and scowled at Charles. But Charles' face seemed it was saying like, 'Keep on doing it and we won't even move an inch until you get one.'

"What's wrong with you?" I shouted in the air and shot another arrow.

As I predicted, it fell again. I was getting furious. I tried another one, and then another, and another, but I couldn't make it near the mark.

Tears full of anger started to pour down my cheeks, but I couldn't differentiate my tears from the rain since they were flowing down my face all together. I grabbed another arrow and pulled the string.

"You can do it, Adela. To give you a tip, it's better to aim higher than the mark and pull the string as far as you can."

I pulled the string until my fingers felt like they were going to bleed and aimed a little higher than the target. I took a deep breath and took a shot. Then, I could hear a thud far away. The arrow was exactly thudded into the mark!

My eyes bulged with excitement. "Oh my god!" I screamed with my high-toned voice. "I did it! I did it!"

I jumped up and down, forgetting the fact that I was all wet. Charles laughed at me loudly and came toward me.

"Great job, Adela. Now, let's get inside. You must be freezing. Here, take my jacket."

He took off his jacket and handed it to me. At first, I denied, but he insisted to put his jacket around me. It was a little heavy because of the water.

"Sorry it's too wet, but I just want you to stay warm."

We ran across the field as fast as we could. Charles put his one arm around my shoulder. My heart was beating so fast. I didn't know whether it was because we were running so fast, or because he had his arm around me, but the thing I was certain was that I was starting to like him more.

Change .

No letters no replies; it made me so nervous and worried about what was happening with Jeff. Is he angry at me? Did I write something wrong or mean on my letter? I kept thinking and thinking, but I couldn't think of the proper reason why.

At first, I checked my mailbox once every day, then I checked twice a day, after that I changed to checking it 3 times a day.

Cathy glanced at me and said, "What's wrong with this Jeffrey guy? It's been almost 3 weeks and he's not sending you any letters?"

I didn't say anything.

"I told you, he is a total jerk. I am almost sure that he moved on. He fell in love with the other girl." Lowell said as he munched on the cookies.

I looked at him and took a deep breath.

"No, he is not a jerk and well, I don't mind if he moved on or not. It's weird that he had sent me dozens of letters at first and when I replied to him, he stopped writing letters. It makes me feel kind of worried about what happened to him."

"So, you just think of him as a friend right? You don't mind if he has a new girlfriend?" Lowell asked carefully.

I shrugged. "I mean, yeah. I would rather be happy for him because if he has a new girlfriend he doesn't have to beg on me like this. I felt really bad for him reading his letters."

Lowell stood up from my bed and grinned at me and Cathy. "Okay, I got to go. It's too late. I will see you guys tomorrow."

Cathy stood up as well. "Aww Lowell, why don't you stay for a couple of minutes more?" Cathy begged.

Lowell smiled at her with his cute dimple on his cheek. "Sorry Cathy, I'm too tired right now. Maybe you guys should have a girl-talk since it has been a long time not doing girl-talk on your own." He made a funny face and made the quotation mark with his fingers. We laughed and waved him goodbye.

I looked at Cathy as he closed the door behind him. "So, how are you doing with Lowell these days? I've been too busy taking care of myself."

Cathy shrugged and sighed deeply. "Not good. He keeps on disappearing. I always try to catch up with him, but he's always like, slipping away from me."

I thought for a minute. "Hey, no offence but, I think you should act more like, outgoing."

Cathy tilted her head. "But I think I am outgoing enough."

"Yeah I know. You are outgoing," I smiled and tapped her back gently. "But I think you are a little too shy in front of Lowell. You should be full of confidence and self-esteem and…you know…"

Cathy sighed again. "I guess you're right. But how can I grab him and stop him from slipping away?"

"Maybe you should ask him right after dinner, something like, 'Hey

Lowell, I was thinking of walking around the garden right now. Wanna join?' or 'Hey Lowell, I love you so much that I want to go out with you and leave a kiss on your sweet darling face.'"

Cathy laughed hard as I made a silly face mimicking Lowell's warm manly voice.

"Haha I like the first one. Thanks for helping me Adela," She said. "Hey, and I'm just curious…How are you doing with Charles?"

I thought for a moment. "Well, hardworking and always training of course."

Cathy squinted her eyes at me. "You know that's not what I'm talking about Adela."

I looked at her for a long time and my face started to burn all over. I felt my heart starting to beat faster and faster.

"N…No, we're not that close. We're just in a relationship of…learning and teaching. That's all."

Cathy kept on squinting with her doubtful eyes. "Yeah well, just like that's so true."

I sighed. "Okay, to tell the truth, I feel like I am starting to have a crush on him."

Cathy banged her fist on the table. "Yes, I knew it. There's no way you can get away with that handsome prince. How's he like to you?"

I giggled excitedly. "He's so nice to me these days. Once he told me that I'm so beautiful. That made my heart to explode like boom!"

Cathy jumped up and down excitedly. "Oh my god, that's so cute! I wish I can hear those kinds of words from Lowell…"

I shrugged. "I am sorry. I should have taken care of you guys more. I feel like I am slipping away from you both."

Cathy smiled. "It's totally fine with me and Lowell. We both understand you need to work hard in order to accomplish your quest. Don't worry about us. We're here to assist you."

As I heard her words, I felt like my heart was getting warmer and it started to beat faster. I made a full smile at my lovely best friend. "Thanks Cathy," I said. "You are the best. And now, we should think of a plan to make Lowell attracted to you."

Cathy nodded and squinted her eyes as she was thinking. I clicked my fingers. "I know he likes books, so why don't you take him out to the national library of Elsmiere? I'll ask Charles where it is and tell you the exact location. And then you can ask him to go with you, and he'll totally say yes to that, wouldn't he?"

Cathy's face started to contort into a smile. "That's a good idea! It's perfect! In that way he and I will have a plenty of time to talk with each other! Thank you so much Adela, it's so nice of you to always help me with my crush problems."

I poked her tummy and giggled. "But first, you should lose weight. Look at your belly! Are you pregnant or what?"

"Adela!" She laughed and pretended to hit me on the head.

I learned so many skills for the past 2 months staying in Elsmiere. I learned how to shoot with bow and arrow, but I didn't quite master it, I also learned riding on horses, fighting with the sword, and using shields. I mastered almost every one of them, except shooting arrows while riding on the horse.

It was the last thing that I had to master before I could actually go out to fight Vulgarians. I practiced step by step following Charles' teaching.

At first, when I was sure that I mastered bow and arrow, I went up onto Beauty and made it walk gently as I grabbed my bow and arrow and try to shoot the target. When I got used to that, I made Beauty sprint a little bit and I would try to get my arrow on the target. I made Beauty run faster as I slowly got used to shooting arrows as I ride on her. As I trained myself, Charles was always there to check if I was okay.

Today, I decided to make her run as fast as she could to feel the realism of the war. I felt my heart pound in my chest as I received the bow and arrow from my maids.

"Good luck again today your majesty." They curtsied and ran off from me.

My hands were getting sweaty and it started to feel slimy on the surface of the bow. But I grabbed onto it more tightly.

Charles ran across the field toward me and tapped my shoulder.

"You are doing really good, Adela. But don't take it too hard on yourself. We can go slowly. Remember we have plenty of time left. Got it?"

"Got it." I said firmly and squeezed the rein with my left hand and my bow with my right hand. I inhaled and let my Beauty sprint across the yard. She had her eyes fixed forward as she was never going to stop. As I felt her determination, I pulled the string of the bow with my fingers slung onto the arrow and the string. I kept my eyes focused on the round flat board with different colors in each part. I had to aim for the red part in the very center of the board. I took a deep breath and waited for the right moment.

A little closer...my voice rang and rang in my mind as I heard my Beauty swung across with her feet rumbling in the speed of a lightning.

I suddenly caught the perfect moment and released my fingers and let go of the arrow. The arrow swished and thudded on the board, but it was way far from the right middle. The arrow was on the black part. My heart fluttered.

"Oh my god! Oh my god!" I yelled in my hyper tone. But my cry made my Beauty overreact. She swayed her front legs in the air and made me crash onto the floor.

"Argh!" I screamed in pain. I heard Charles running and screaming my name several times.

"Adela, are you okay? Oh you stupid horse!"

"Don't...don't blame the horse..." I said and moaned as I felt the incredible pain in my left ankle. "Ouch, that really hurts."

I saw my two maids rushing towards me and sat down on their knees. Charles sat on the grass and grabbed my left leg gently.

"Adela, I should check if your leg is all right. First stretch your legs out in front of me…yes that's it…now tell me where you feel pain the most."

I pointed at my left ankle as I kept moaning and moaning.

"Okay, you'll be fine. Don't worry. Are you able to move your ankle? Stretch out your left foot, can you…?"

I tried to stretch it out. It slightly moved as I beared the pain and did as he told me to do.

Charles nodded patiently. "Well, it barely moves, but still it can move. That means your ankle is not broken, thank god. You've just sprained your ankle."

Phew, I sighed in relief. If I had broken my ankle, I would have had to take the rest for a long time, which will delay our set-off.

"Would you like some water your highness?" One of the maids handed me a bottle of cool water. I received it and opened the lid. The icy surface of the water met my lips and ran down my throat. I felt much better. I closed the lid and handed it back to her. "Thanks." I said.

Charles stared at me, worried. "Are you all right? Do you need some rest?"

I tried to stand up slowly as I can, not moving my muscle in my left foot, but I fell down as I felt a huge pain surging on my ankle.

"Argh!" I groaned again. Charles helped me stand up from where I was by having his arm around my shoulders, so I can stand up easily. Finally

I stood up and tried to get on Beauty again. But Charles grabbed my shoulders.

"No no no no... you are going to hurt yourself. Don't you have to take a rest for a moment and get some ice on your ankle?"

I hesitated and called the maid who was holding the icy cold water bottle that I drank a minute ago. I received the bottle from her and crouched my back and put the bottle on my ankle and stood like that for a few seconds. Then I stood up and handed it back to the maid.

I grinned at Charles. "There, satisfied?"

Charles looked astonished and didn't say a thing. He quietly brought the steel stairs and put it between the Beauty and me so I can climb up the stairs and up to my Beauty again. When I finally got up on her again, I patted her soft neck and stroked her mane.

"You're doing great Beauty." I said and hugged her neck gently. Then I received the bow and arrow from Charles and stared into his eyes.

"I'm all right. I am not using my ankle during horse riding, so no worries, okay?"

Charles nodded and smiled. My heart started thumping as my Beauty slowly rumbled her feet towards the aim. I squeezed the rein and slapped it. She started to run faster and faster as I prepared to shoot at the board. When the perfect moment came, I released the arrow. I could only hear my heart pounding as if it were going to explode.

The arrow struck on the board making a thud sound. I pulled the rein and stopped.

The arrow was right inside the very middle circle.

"Oh my god!" I squealed but I quickly covered my mouth, so my Beauty wouldn't overreact. I turned to Charles excitedly.

He was smiling as usual and his mouth seemed like screaming, 'Way to go Adela!' at me.

I soon got off the horse and stood on the ground. Charles walked quickly towards me and I stood there watching him blankly. I didn't move an inch as he suddenly hugged me tight in his arms.

"I knew you could make it," He said in his sweet voice. "You've... you've improved so much...so much."

I bet it was the longest hug that I had gotten from Charles, or I should say...it was the first time.

"You've improved so much, Adela. I can't be more impressed."

"Yeah, you've probably said that for like hundred times by now."

Charles and I both laughed as we sat on the bench, taking a long rest, as I apply an ice pack on my ankle. It was swollen just a few minutes ago, but after I cooled it up with the ice, it seemed to be less swollen. Also, the pain was going off slowly.

"How's your ankle now?" Charles asked worriedly. He knelt down in front of me and grabbed the ice from my hand. He slowly rolled the ice pack around my ankle using his right hand and gently held my heel with his left hand. He kept on and on like that for a long time. For that moment, it was so hard for me to breathe as I could look at him more closely. His blonde curly hair was lively and silky. His eyelashes were pretty longer than I expected and his skin was as smooth and pure as ever. His mouth had a pinkish lips and his even teeth was showing a little from his mouth.

His lips seem to move...

"...Hey, Adela. Are you listening?"

I was accidently caught watching by him as his eyes met mine. Oh my goodness, I blushed and looked away from him and moved my eyes to my ankle.

"Uh, yeah sure..." I mumbled.

"Your highness," One of his bodyguards came rushing by and whispered to him. Charles stood up with his smile and held out his hand to me. "Let's go, Adela." He said with his excited voice. "He has finally come! We can't make him wait!"

Him? Who is 'him' he's talking about? Maybe 'him' he's talking about must be someone he mentioned when I was examining his face a minute ago.

I kept on wondering who 'him' would be. Oh, wait...could 'him' be... Jeff?

"There he comes!" Charles exclaimed and stared at the gate.

Far away from where I was standing, there were body guards opening the gate of the castle and behind them...

"Oh my god," I murmured to myself.

I couldn't believe my eyes...it wasn't Jeff.

It was Grandpa Louie.

Good News and Bad News

I stood there, flabbergasted as Grandpa Louie slowly came towards us as he got assisted by the body guards.

"Why is he...?" I tried to say something, but I was too surprised that my mouth could barely move.

"Hello," Grandpa Louie said quietly. "Long time no see...Mr. Jones and Miss Monette..."

"Why are you...?" I couldn't say a word after that.

"Why don't we have dinner together, shall we? I'll tell my mother you're here, Grandpa."

We went inside and to the dining room. I told one of the maids to bring Cathy and Lowell to have dinner. The maid ran off and called them immediately and they both arrived at the dining room. They saw Grandpa Louie and both made their mouth a shape like an 'o'.

"Oh my god, you're here!" Cathy jumped up and down and hugged Grandpa Louie. Grandpa Louie held her with his arms and hugged her back. "Oh my, your name was...uh...Miss...I am sorry. What was your name again?"

"It's Catherine Middleton, sir." She said smiling.

"Oh, yes Catherine...and that handsome friend of Adela over there...I remember your name was Lo...Low..."

"Lowell Henderson, sir. Nice meeting you again. We missed you so much Grandpa Louie."

We all sat down around the table and waited for the food to be delivered from the kitchen. Grandpa Louie looked around the room and seemed amazed.

"Your house looks just wonderful, Charles." He complimented.

"Well thank you very much, sir. We changed the interior of this room right after your last visit."

"Oh, I didn't notice that."

Suddenly the door opened and the Queen came in. Queen Georgina made a huge smile on her face and walked in with Olivianna.

"Oh, my fellow Mr. McCarthy, welcome again!" Queen hugged him gently and sat down. So did Olivianna.

"Olivianna, you seem to have grown taller than I saw you last time I came here." He said.

Olivianna blushed and looked down. Everyone in that room laughed. "Is your father here from Anastelon yet?" Grandpa Louie turned to Charles.

"No. My father is not here nor at Anastelon. He's off to visit other countries. He's quite busy these days, but he'll come back soon as you came to our country."

"Dinner is to be served!" The chef from the kitchen yelled and the waiters burst open the door and delivered the dishes. For the appetizer, we had cold salad with herb dressings and tomatoes smothered with mozzarella cheese. It was delicious, especially the soft cheese and fresh tomatoes. Grandpa Louie told us that the tomatoes were brought from Devina, and that's why they taste so fresh.

For the main dish, they served us Lamb stew on each of our plates. It was savory and tasty. The meat was so soft and chewy and it was not much different from chicken. Whenever I chewed on it, the savory juice oozed out of it and smeared my tongue with its amazing taste.

"It tastes great as it seems." Grandpa Louie said as he swallowed his first bite.

In that time, I kept wondering the reason why Grandpa Louie came to Elsmiere. Maybe he brought some news from Devina…or did Jeffrey send him to tell how awful he feels? I chewed and chewed as I daydreamed about all the reasons I could come up with.

"Psst! Adela," Lowell, next to me whispered. "Are you all right? You seem kind of…"

I looked up and smiled at him blankly. I shook my head. "No, nothing. I was just…daydreaming."

Lowell kept glancing at me worriedly as I continued devouring all the food. Then we had herb and tangerine pudding for dessert.

Grandpa Louie opened his mouth again. "I am aware that you heard from Charles why I came here, sweetheart." He slowly let out his words in his unique accent. I glanced at Charles and turned to Grandpa Louie. I couldn't tell him that I didn't catch what Charles said, so I just nodded, biting my lips.

Grandpa Louie stood up from his seat and said, "Shall we go, then?"

Lowell and Cathy left us while we were heading to the garden. Charles told me that we are going to have a cup of tea with him to talk over it.

Talk about what? I was starting to get nervous like the moment I was getting the grades in school.

???

I was having all the question marks filling my brain. I was feeling anxious and curious at the same time as I didn't know what Grandpa Louie was up to. But as soon as we arrived in the garden and sat down around the tea table, he opened his mouth.

"You may have not known, Adela," He took a deep breath and exhaled. "That I am half-blooded."

I shrugged confusedly. "Oh, okay."

What is he up to with half-blood? I mean, there are a lot of people who are half-blooded in the world. I waited for his next speech, feeling confused.

"I am half Devina and half Aian." He added.

I thought for a moment. And my jaw dropped.

"Wa…wait…that means you are…like our family? You have our blood?"

"Well, half, exactly."

"Then can you transform into animals like us?" I asked with my eyes wide open.

"Sadly no, but half-bloods have their own special talents," he said. "Even if they don't belong to any of those two."

I glanced at both Charles and Grandpa Louie and shook my head.

"Oh, then what's your specialty?" I asked.

Grandpa Louie's eyes widened and glanced at Charles and back at me. "Oh, Charles, didn't you tell her why I am here for?"

There was a short silence. I just didn't say anything since I didn't catch what Charles told me earlier.

Grandpa Louie continued. "I can read people's bloods," He said. "When I hold anyone's wrist, I can feel and hear their blood swishing through their veins. I can feel the beat of their heart pumping out blood. So I am here to analyze your blood and check if your two lives are still okay in there and what you're going to transform into when you train to transform."

I nodded. "Wow, is that even possible? That's amazing." I exclaimed. "But my mother told me that I still have two lives available inside me, and there were no risks in my life that may have occurred me to death."

Grandpa Louie reached out his wrinkly hands. "Well, no one knows honey. Now please can I have your hand for a second?"

I swallowed and gave him my right hand. He softly grabbed my wrist with his both hands and closed his eyes. He squeezed my wrist gently as he inhaled. I could feel my heart beating faster as he just stayed like that frozen for a long time. A long moment passed but he still didn't move an inch.

I started to feel more confused and nervous. I slowly turned my head to Charles, who was staring at my wrist, frozen like Grandpa Louie. I whispered to him. "Pssp, Charles, is he doing all right?"

Charles let in a short breath as if he was surprised and looked at me. He squinted at me and made a sign at me to shut up. I scowled and turned back to Grandpa Louie, who was still reading my blood. But as the time passed, his facial expression seemed to turn weirder and weirder.

For that moment I wished I could read his mind and see what he was seeing in my blood.

Suddenly, Grandpa Louie's eyes opened. He stared at mine for a long time and finally opened his mouth.

"Adela," His lips trembled. "You just have one life left."

PART 3

Charles

"You can have someone way
better than him,
someone who cares about you
and loves you more than anything,
someone who loves you in a proper
way, not just requiring you for love"

Secrets

No one would believe that I had thought myself to be gay before I met Adela. My mother and father also even thought that I was gay and tried to hide my 'dirty secret'-they call it- and I was always intimidated by myself because my parents were always worried that I wouldn't get married when I become the king. While my friends were hanging out with their loving girl friends, I hung out with my best friend Lucinda. She is the first person, besides my parents, to know that I thought myself to be gay at that time. But she accepted my secret and told me that there's no difference.

"Why so squished huh?" She poked me prankishly. "Everyone around you is jealous of you. You are the prince of this country. You should wake up from your fear Charles."

She always used to tell me this and as she was with me the whole time, I felt like I was feeling better and better. But she was not the one who I could get my heart beating.

I tried so hard to get my heart beat for a girl I like, but for years I couldn't find any. Or, possibly, one of the biggest reasons could be that I had to be in protection as the prince of this country, and as a result I couldn't get in a proper relationship with any girls. So I had just accepted the fact that I was gay after all.

But when I met Adela in Anastelon, I was dazzled by her beauty.

Her sparkling eyes, lovely smile, gorgeous dress...I still remember her stunning blue satin dress that she wore on the day we first met...my heart was throbbing as if it was going to explode. The more I spent time with her, the more she came across my mind. Then I realized...I was falling straightly in love with her.

I think I know why that Jeff guy is into Adela so much. Adela has this kind of mysterious charm that pulls guys' minds. And I am one of the guys who is attracted to this lovely girl.

And I would do anything to get her to stay with me.

Do you or do you not?

The quest could continue if these three conditions are satisfied.

The first condition is that the princess should be trained for an ample time with the highly professional trainer and should be allowed by princess' trainer to continue on the rest of the quest.

The second condition is that the princess should be in strict protection just in case. So my father is travelling around other countries to help Adela's army gain more soldiers. That means we are going to have double protection and double security for our precious princess.

The last condition, which is the most important part, is that the princess, who might have the blood of an Aian, should make sure that she has two lives so she would be safe during the battle. However, if the princess doesn't, it becomes a huge problem.

"I can't believe it," Adela mumbled as she kept walking in a circle. "This is totally impossible. When did I lose my first life? My father and mother would have told me about that if they have known this."

I sighed and stared into the distance blankly. My words were lost as I was too shocked hearing that from Grandpa Louie. Is that really true? I asked that question for about hundred times, but Grandpa Louie lowered his head and nodded with his face hardened.

Everything was going smooth, but I'd never expected such a big problem and neither did Adela. Then do we have to cancel the quest and go back to normal? Wait…does that mean Adela and I should be apart like before?

My mind couldn't stop bubbling out the worst things that could happen to both of us. Suddenly I lifted my head as I heard Adela stop.

"Oh," She exhaled and gently turned to me.

"Hey, I think…I have a hunch." She said carefully.

I barely could move my lips. "What?" I murmured.

"I was once told by my father that I fell from the tower when I was 4 years old."

"How tall was the tower?"

"Well, according to my memory it had about two thousand stairs, so it was quite tall. But the doctor told my parents that I just broke some parts of my body and I was lucky that I still had two lives. My parents couldn't believe it at first because the tower was too tall…"

I swallowed and continued listening.

"…and I am thinking maybe, this was when I used up my first life."

"Are you sure? Do you have any more life-taking moments that you doubt to have lost your life?"

Adela thought for a moment and shook her head. "No, that was the most dangerous moment. Our family powered up the protection and doubled the security from then on."

I sighed and nodded. "Well, that must be it then."

"Do I have to…give up the quest?" Adela asked hesitantly.

I stared at her eyes and stood up from where I was sitting. I slowly approached her, smiling. My heart was pounding wildly as I hugged her in my arms. She seemed to be frozen by my sudden action. The smell of shampoo danced under my nostrils. Her incredible scent was making me dizzy and bewitched.

I brushed my hand down her back. "Nope," I whispered. "Everything is up to you, princess. If you want to keep going, we can keep going. No matter how many lives you have. I can't be bothered to tell my mother about this, but we have to tell her."

I gently loosed my arms that were around her and held her shoulders with my hands. I could feel the slight shudder as our eyes met. She looked so cute when she swallowed nervously and looked away shyly. She kept sliding her fingers through her silky hair as the awkwardness filled the air. I looked down and chuckled.

I opened my mouth. "Hey, Adela…Do you want to…?"

The phone ring pierced the air. We both stared at the phone and then at each other. Adela slowly walked toward the phone and lifted it. She stood like that for quite a few second. During the phone call, she just murmured "yes" continuously. As the phone call ended, she turned at me.

"Grandpa Louie is leaving in just half an hour," She said. "But before that, he wants to tell me something…"

She swallowed and bit her lips nervously.

"…He wants to talk to me about Jeffrey."

"Jeffrey?"

I almost lost my control, but I quickly calmed myself down. I smiled at her and nodded.

"By yourself or should I come along with you...?" I asked patiently.

"I know you'd feel distracted...but can you come with me? I need someone to...you know...rely on."

Rely on...that word felt so magical to me. She wants to rely on me. She sees me like someone she can rely on. It feels weird...in a good way.

We rushed to the garden where Grandpa Louie was at. He was still enjoying tea as if he had forgotten that he told Adela the bad news. He looked ever so peaceful and relaxed. We sat around the tea table just like before. Grandpa Louie turned his head to us and put his tea cup down.

"Hello again my dears," He said. "I just wanted to speak to you privately."

I signed to the guards and the maids to give us some private time. As they all left, Grandpa Louie started speaking.

"You know that boy Jeffrey?" He started off. I could hear Adela swallow.

"I heard that he asked you to be his girlfriend. Is that right?"

Adela nodded silently.

"Well, his father Mr. Thomson...he is an acquaintance of mine...and we usually bump into each other, so I heard some news about his son Jeffrey. At first he told me that his son changed completely after you left. And Mr. Thomson said that he thinks it's because his son Jeffrey was broken-hearted. He suffered too much after you left him like that. Jeff used to help his dad a lot with making wines, but he stopped helping. So Mr. Thomson had harsh times doing all the work by himself. His son locked himself in his room and only came out once a day with an envelope in his hand."

"I guess those envelopes he was holding were the letters that he was going to send to Adela, weren't they?" I asked.

"Well, yes." Grandpa Louie kept on talking. "He sent letters to you and he never missed a single day. And one day I met Mr. Thomson again and he told me that he had a huge fight with his son because Mr. Thomson couldn't stand him anymore. Mr. Thomson's eyes were teary, I can still remember, he even slapped his face hard, he told me. And then I heard that Jeff left the house in anger and he didn't come home that night."

Adela covered her mouth, looking shocked as ever. Her hands were trembling as she asked carefully.

"Then what happened after that?"

"Well," Grandpa Louie scratched his head and continued. "I don't know what happened next. I rarely saw him coming out of his house. But I exactly remember that whenever he came out, he was definitely bonier and more unenergetic than before. Maybe he has lost his appetite."

I stared at Adela worriedly. She lowered her head down, biting her lips. I patted her back with my hand.

It felt weird to me that I couldn't feel any sympathy towards that Jeffrey guy. Instead, I felt really worried about Adela. She has to focus on her quest…and focus on me rather than that country boy.

"Adela..." Grandpa Louie sighed deeply. "This may be tough for you to accept, but as an acquaintance of Jeffrey I should ask you this..."

Grandpa Louie sighed again and opened his mouth. "Can't you just... accept his confession?"

My heart dropped. I quickly turned my eyes to Adela. Her eyes were widened and her whole body seemed to be frozen.

"I know, sweetheart. As a princess of a country, it would be hard to choose someone you can rely on," Grandpa Louie added. "But, Jeffrey is a nice man as you'd already know, and you can rely on him. I can guarantee that."

Still, Adela didn't say anything. She kept her head down and seemed so nervous. I decided to say something to her, but she lifted her head up.

"Yes...he is a really nice gentleman." Adela nodded and grinned. "I am so sorry Grandpa Louie, I think I should go up and uh...anyway, I'll see you tomorrow..."

"Adela sweetie, I am leaving right now."

"...I'll see you someday then. It was nice hearing about Jeffrey again. Please tell him that I miss him Grandpa..."

We all stood up from our seats and I watched Adela open her arms for a hug with Grandpa Louie. They gave each other a long gentle hug and Grandpa Louie turned to me. He gave me a hug and disappeared out of the garden.

I looked at Adela again. Her face was totally unreadable. Grandpa Louie offered her to accept Jeffrey's confession, but Adela avoided replying to him. What is she going to do about Jeffrey? Is she going to accept him like Grandpa Louie said? Oh no…please…that can't happen. Should I ask her about what she's going to do?

Adela turned her face to me and smiled with her eyes teary. "Let's go up to our rooms shall we?" She said with her voice trembling.

We both didn't say a word. We went up the stairs and arrived in front of Adela's room. She gave me a big smile, trying to hide her tears in her eyes. Her hand waved me goodbye.

"I've got to go, I think I need some time to think…today was such a horrifying day for me…" She mumbled absent-mindedly.

"Okay, Adela. You should take some rests, and don't think too much about what you heard today. It'll get your concentration hazy. Also, call me whenever you need help. All right?" I said.

She nodded and slowly closed her door. I stood there staring into space as my mind kept rewinding back to the words that Grandpa Louie said. Those words kept ranging inside my brain.

There is no way she is dating with Jeffrey…There should be…

Do you have Jeffrey in your mind or do you not?

No

"Hey, Adela. Are you there?"

It was only 5 o'clock in the morning. I knocked on her door really softly but still loud enough to wake her up. I already rang her room for three times, but she wouldn't answer me, so I came all over to her room to wake her up.

"Come on, Adela. Are you crying over again?" I whispered while I got my mouth attached to the door gap. "Please Adela, can't you open this door..."

"Excuse me, your highness. May I ask what you are doing, sir?"

I jumped as a maid sneaked by behind me. I turned around and smiled awkwardly.

"Well, I...was just trying to wake the princess up. It's my job to train her so..." I mumbled.

"Oh, do you mean princess Monette, sir?" The maid nodded. "She is already awakened, sir."

"Oh, is that true? Then where has she gone to?"

"She is in the makeup room, your highness. I heard it from other maids a few minutes ago before I came up here."

"All right. Thank you very much."

I left running down the hallway and down the stairs to the makeup room. The hallway was dark and chilly and there were hardly bright lights shining down the hallway. I turned quickly as I reached the corner. I could see a string of orange light spreading out on the marble floor. As I got closer and closer to the makeup room, my head was bubbling up with so many thoughts. Why is she at the makeup room? Why is she awakened so early? Do the artists have something to do with Jeffrey guy? I couldn't control the crazy thoughts filling in my head. I got closer and closer to the light and as it came near, I slowed down my feet and adjusted my breath. My lungs were as if they were on fire, but it didn't matter. After I came around, I was standing directly in front of the door. My heart started drumming inside me as I grabbed the doorknob. The door made a creaking sound as I pulled it slightly. I peeked through the gap.

I could see a few artists standing around one chair in the corner and on the chair, there was somebody. That somebody must be Adela, I thought and stepped inside.

Everyone turned their heads to me and somebody on the chair leaned and turned her head to see who had come. My jaw dropped as our eyes met.

There was Adela on the chair, but she didn't look the same as yesterday. Something has changed in her appearance, and that something was her hair. Her silky brown hair used to smooth down to her waist, but now the tips of her hair ended just above her shoulders, curled up nicely. I stood there stupidly until she opened her mouth to speak.

"Hey, Charles." She smiled at me awkwardly. "Were you looking for me?"

My head went blank and didn't know what to say.

"Nice hair." I blurted out at last.

Adela smiled in her own kind of way that I loved. She blushed a little.

"Thanks, well what's up?"

"What's up?" I said agitatedly. "That's what I want to ask you, Adela, really, what is up?"

Adela stood up from her seat.

"Well, I was really horrified after I heard some news yesterday…" She fidgeted and took a step toward me. "And I decided to cut my hair, for refreshing my mind and everything."

I stared at her confusedly. Suddenly, one of the artists behind her clicked her fingers.

"Your highness, sir. To say, it is a girls' thing," She smiled as she tried to explain. "Sometimes girls need refreshment for example, after breaks, exams, horror movies, or after getting huge amount of stress!"

"Yes, sir. It's like a meaning of 'starting new and fresh'." Another artist added.

I moved my eyes around her beautiful curly hair. Her hair got shorter, that was all, but looking at her felt different. She even looked cuter and sophisticated than before. It felt like the moment that I had to add some words of praises like, 'Wow, Adela, you look so gorgeous, or that hairstyle fits you perfectly', but I couldn't. I just stood there, nodding and smiling awkwardly.

Adela turned her eyes from the mirror to me and giggled.

"What are you doing you fool! You look just like a designer who just cut my hair, examining if it's fine."

I stopped smiling and gently squeezed her shoulder and whispered, "Adela, can I talk to you for a second?"

She seemed to be frozen for a second and stood up.

We went out to the hall way. The marble floor lost its shininess as she closed the door behind her. She seemed to be smiling, but I could notice a little hint of anxiety behind her smile.

I let out a long deep breath and opened my mouth.

"Adela, I know it doesn't feel good talking about this, but I should ask you anyway…" I started as I stared directly to her eyes. "I was worried after seeing you crying when Grandpa Louie was here yesterday. What are you going to do about…it?"

Contrary to my expectations, she kept smiling and maintained her confidence. She shrugged.

"What are you talking about?" She pretended that she knew nothing.

"Come on. He asked you to accept Jeffrey's confession. What are you going to say to that?"

The words that were blocked inside my head blurted out fast as I couldn't stand anymore. I needed to know what she was up to.

But she shrugged instead and walked down the hallway.

Then she turned around and smiled at me and said,

"It's up to what I choose right?"

"You are not going to tell me, huh?" I shouted as I followed around Adela, who kept her mouth shut for hours. She seemed to enjoy having me around like this. She kept giggling to herself as she ran away from me.

"I told you Charles. We need to protect each other's privacy! It's a secret. I wouldn't even tell Cathy or Lowell. So I can't tell you, either."

"But I am more than that to you Adela." I accidently blurted out the words I wasn't supposed to.

"Well, what are you to me?" She looked at me strangely.

I had to cover up my speech as fast as I could.

"Um…uh…I am your trainer as well as a bodyguard, so I have the right to know." I said quickly.

"Very funny, Charles. You know you are being so childish right now. Now, go back to your room. I wouldn't have let you in my room if I had known you would hang onto me like this."

"I won't hang onto you if you just tell me how you are going to treat him."

"Wait. First, let me ask you. Why is this so important to you?"

"Well, because it is…"

Suddenly, there was a knock on the door. Adela rushed to the door and opened it. She had a conversation with someone whoever was behind the door and turned back to me.

"I'm sorry, Charles. My family left a call just a few minutes ago. I'll be back soon okay?"

I waved her goodbye and waited until the door was closed behind her. Then I started opening the drawers and look keenly on the shelves as fast as I could. I couldn't give up. I had to know what was happening in her head. There must be a letter that she was going to send to Jeffrey for the reply on his stupid confession.

Why is he always blocking my way? This was mean of me, but that moment I really wished that he wasn't even alive. If Adela says yes, I'm going to kill him, I thought as I looked and looked.

Suddenly I spotted a hot pink spring note that seemed just like a diary that Adela would write on. I carefully opened the diary, being wary of when she'll burst inside while I am reading this. I skimmed through the pages and opened the latest page that Adela wrote on.

July 25th Wednesday

It was just yesterday's note. My eyes rolled down and stopped at the words written in simple, bold letters, seemingly because she wrote with her hands full of tension. It was not even a full sentence, and those words made my heart pound.

The words lay,

Jeffrey...Yes

Lowell

'Cling clang'; the glasses bumped each other as the reddish purple wine wobbled. I took a huge sip and I could feel the coolness of the wine running down my throat.

"Hey, this wine reminds me of Jeffrey. He and his father produce wonderful wine, and I think this tastes similar to the ones that they make."

Adela's comment felt like a stab on my heart. It kept pounding so hard inside my chest as if it were going to blow up. I had to grab the fork and put some ravioli inside my mouth, but I couldn't because I knew my hand was going to wobble just like the wine I drank a minute ago.

"Charles, what's up? Why aren't you eating?" Adela asked worriedly.

I looked up and made a fake smile at her. "I am not that hungry. I had some snack before I came down here, so…"

"Wait a minute…did you steal my snacks from the drawer?" Adela said with her voice slightly louder. "Your face seemed like you've done something wrong after I came back from phone call."

"Wait. You guys were together?" Lowell cut in.

"Manners, my dears!" My mother's voice pierced through our conversation. "Charles, it's too bad that you wouldn't like to have dinner with us tonight. I'll send a maid with you to your room. Anna?"

One of the maids gently walked toward me and curtsied.

We left the dining room and walked down the hall.

"Oh," I turned to the maid. "Anna, I'd like a bottle of cider, cool and fresh. Would you get that for me?"

"As you order, your highness." She curtsied and headed to the kitchen.

"Please bring it to the second floor terrace." I shouted at her back.

The damp breeze swished around my hair. My eyes were lost by the cascades of stars and the moon, looking like a boat that was floating on the sea of darkness. The cider tasted so sweet and I didn't want the taste on my tongue to go away.

The cider tastes better than wine, I thought to myself. Maybe I should change my favorite beverage from wine to cider. It's not that bad.

Suddenly, the door behind me creaked open. "Whoa," Someone behind me let out a startled murmur. "I didn't know you were here."

I jumped up from my seat and spinned around. There was Lowell, standing behind the door. He seemed as if he was going to leave, but I stopped him.

"No. Wait. You can come in, Mr. Henderson, or should I call you... Lowell?"

He seemed a little hesitant, but he smiled awkwardly and stepped inside. He sat down on the other side of the chair. I offered him a drink of cider.

"So, how's everything in here huh?" I started off the conversation.

Lowell bit his lips and seemed shy. He hesitated for a while and answered. "Well, it can't be any more peaceful than this."

We both sipped from our cider and stared into space vacantly.

I couldn't stand this awkwardness anymore, so I decided to be more outgoing.

"Hey you know what?" I broke into the silence and said. "We are the only boys in same age, and we're both on helping Adela on her quest, and we haven't even talked to each other since the start,"

Lowell slightly shrugged and nodded, showing his concurrence.

"And do you know what I did when I had a friend who I want to get closer to?" I continued as I saw him shrugging again. "I proposed that we should share secrets with each other. Just one each and after we told each other a secret, actually, that made us really close."

Lowell stared at me strangely like he didn't know what I was talking about.

"I know it is really childish and stupid…but it helps…Do you want to share secrets?" I offered him carefully.

Lowell seemed to think for a minute, but he nodded at last.

"Okay then, why don't you tell me first? Do you have something that you can spill?"

"Well…" Lowell thought. "I do have one, but it's quite a big one and I am not sure if I can trust you…"

"Trust me, Lowell. Your secret will be safe with me. I promise."

"Okay then," He sighed and opened his mouth. "Well, I don't know how you're going to accept this, but…well…I hid the letters."

"What letters?"

"The letters from Devina…you know…that guy Jeffrey?"

My jaw dropped. "…What?" I yelled.

"I've been sneaking in the mail room and collecting them." He continued.

"Since when?"

"Since you stopped stealing them."

"Jesus, I can't believe it…but why?"

He seemed a little surprised at my question. He paused and opened his mouth again.

"Well, I guess I didn't like seeing Adela crying over those weird letters. I just couldn't stand it."

"Wow," I clapped in excitement. "There's finally someone who thinks the same as I do."

"What's yours?" He asked curiously. "I bet you started this because you have something big to spill, don't you?"

"Haha," I chuckled. "To be honest, I do have a secret to tell, but I am not sure how you are going to react to this…"

"What is it? Tell me." He said excitedly.

I couldn't move my lips easily as if they were stuck together with glue. I finally opened my mouth. "I am being so honest with you…I actually… have a crush on Adela."

As I shut my mouth and glanced at Lowell's face, his face seemed to be hardened. He didn't move an inch or say anything. I was worried if he was too shocked to hear my words.

"Are you okay? What's wrong?" I asked.

He just didn't say anything. He had been looking at me with a big smile on his face before I told my secret, but after that he looked away from me as his smile disappeared.

I tried to tap his shoulder to be friendly, but he avoided me before I could get my hand on.

"I'm sorry," He said finally, without eye contact. "That was rude of me. I'm just…really shocked to hear what you've just said…"

"I know right?" I continued. "But I am sure you know how amazing she is. She mesmerizes everyone beside her. I just can't understand how you and Adela can stay as just friends. If I were you I'd fall for her and confess to her right away."

Lowell sighed and didn't say anything.

I tapped his back to be as friendly as I could. "Hey I think this made us a lot closer to each other. Don't you think so? I feel like I've got a special friend just now."

"Yeah, special." He mumbled, looking down.

We both stood up from our seats and opened the door. We left the terrace leaving the stars in the sky behind.

And back then, I didn't know such a terrible thing was going to happen to all of us.

Shattered into Fragments

It was three days left before the ball night opens. The invitations were already sent. And the lasting three days was the period for them to prepare for the ball; buying their dresses and suits, getting carriages reserved for them to get to the castle, and most importantly, looking for partners. I had been thinking how I was going to ask Adela to be my partner, but I was afraid.

Those bold letters kept appearing on my eyes.

'Yes...' 'Yes...' 'Yes...' Yes...'

I shook my head to erase the word. This was just so obvious. She was going to accept that stupid guy. Maybe she is already falling for him. Maybe she already has liked him and the tears she dropped were the meaning of her love towards Jeffrey. Or maybe she has already sent the letter and they are already dating each other.

"No," I jumped up from my desk and inhaled. "I've got to stop her."

I dragged the chair and got out from the seat. I sprinted to the door and stepped out my room. I ran across the hall way and arrived in front of Adela's room. I calmed myself down and knocked on the door. My heart was throbbing inside my chest, so hard that it felt so heavy. I waited. But she didn't come out.

I knocked again patiently, but again there was no reply.

"Where is she?" I whispered to myself and swallowed.

I looked over my both sides of the hall, but there was no one. I nervously wandered around a little bit and sighed.

"Maybe I should go look for her."

It was the time when I just decided to go downstairs to look for her. Suddenly, I heard thumping footsteps coming from the stairs across the hall way.

I bet that's she, I thought and headed to the stairs.

The steps rang throughout the whole floor and when it sounded like it finally reached the second floor, I could see the silhouette of the noisemaker.

"Adela!" I shouted in excitement. "I was looking for you. Where have you..."

"How could you do this, Charles?" There was Adela, screaming and swinging something on her left hand.

"What is it?" I tried to grab and see what she was holding.

"Don't," She screamed louder. "Don't touch it you thief!"

"What's wrong?" I asked, horrified.

"Huh, do you know you are really good at pretending Charles?" She yelled. "Such a good, good actor."

"Adela wait. Stop!" Her friends Cathy and Lowell caught up with her and stood behind her. I glanced at them and asked, "What have I done wrong? Can you guys...tell me?"

"I'm sick of you lying to me like this!" Adela yelled at me as her tears streamed down her face. "It's your entire fault. Why are you so selfish? You thought you can stop me from getting mails from Jeffrey if you just steal them away from me?"

"Wait, what?" I said as I suddenly realized what was happening. "The letters…that are from Devina?"

"Stop pretending! I knew it was you. I shouldn't have trusted you on this. I should have known how selfish you are and I should have…"

"No no no, you are totally mistaken." I interrupted. "It was not me. It was Lowell who stole them."

But she didn't seem to believe what I just said. "Do you think I am that stupid?" She snorted in anger. "It was Lowell who kindly found out what you did. He told me that he saw you sneaking inside the mailroom and spotted you getting my letters."

"Wait, I've never…"

"And do you know where he got these letters from?" She yelled even louder. "He told me that he sneaked inside your room and got these, for me to see what you have done."

I stared at blankly at the letters, and then I glared sharply at Lowell. Our eyes met, but he glared at me back as if he has done nothing wrong. I snorted as my anger grew up.

"How dare you tell her that I did it? Why the heck would you do this to me?" I raised my voice and stepped toward Lowell.

"How dare you growl at him like that you freak!" Adela shouted as she stood in front of Lowell to protect him.

"Adela, step aside. This is between me and Lowell." I said to her calmly, but she didn't move an inch.

"This is between you and me." Adela insisted.

"So you completely believe that I am the thief?" I asked her with my voice lowered.

"I cannot believe you are still asking as if..."

"Fine," I cut in and said. "I stole them. But you know what Adela? You should be aware that you have a liar as your best friend, and I am extremely disappointed in both you and Lowell." I snapped and walked away from them. I could hear her yelling at me at my back, but her voice faded away.

Three days were left before the ball night opened. The invitations were already sent. And the lasting three days was the period for us to prepare for the ball; buying dresses and suits, getting carriages reserved to get to the castle, and most importantly, looking for partners.

And this was not a good start for all of us.

I calmed down my headache and tried to breathe slowly to slower my heartbeat. It was beating crazily inside of me. The moment kept appearing in front of my eyes, and I couldn't feel more terrible than that.

But first, I couldn't understand that Lowell guy, and I still couldn't believe that he told her that I was the thief. Maybe he was afraid of himself getting caught and making Adela angry. But he couldn't just tell her that I did what he did.

That moment, I really wanted to kill him and strangle him to death, but I had to calm down for Adela. Ugh, why are guys around me so incomprehensible? I thought he was a gentleman, but he was no different with that country boy.

I have to get Adela back before the ball, I thought. But…how?

I thought and thought, but I couldn't get the right answer for this. I needed someone to help me, and that thought reminded me of my old friend, Lucinda.

Lucinda was my friend (as I mentioned in the first place) who always took care of me as friends and we were so close to each other that we called each other twins when we were young. But now, it has been a long time not contacting each other since I was busy doing training with Adela.

Maybe she could help me, I thought and I lifted the phone and dialed her number. After a couple of series of tones, she answered.

"Hello." She said with her soft voice.

"Hey, this is Charles." I said calmly.

"Oh my goodness, Charlie!" She squealed in joy. "It's been a long time not hearing from you. How's everything?"

"Why do you think I called you, huh?" I laughed.

"What's the problem, Charles? I know of course, you always have called me because you were teased by someone. Who teased you today huh?" She made fun of me just like she always has done since kindergarten.

"No. Come on, Lucy. That was like, in kindergarten. Don't make fun of me. I am not in the mood for that."

"Then tell me what's up."

"Well, it's about this girl…"

I told Lucy everything that has happened with me and Adela. On her side of the phone, she was quietly listening to what I was saying. As I finally finished telling her everything, she giggled.

"Wow, you finally have someone you like, don't you? You know what? You are lucky to have a friend like me, because I know girls well and you don't. I can help you out with this."

"How?"

"Um, Charles first, girls can get bored if you just treat them too well all the time," She commented. "Maybe you should just leave her for this week. Don't touch her nor talk to her."

"Then what about the ball on this week?" I asked. "I want her to be my partner."

"You can have another girl as your partner," She said. "me!"

"You?" I jumped. "Why should I do that?"

"Because girls don't like it when you are always there for her. Sometimes, you should give her some space, so she would know how it is like without you."

"But," I felt my head getting dizzy. "This is my last chance, and I've waited for the ball for ages to finally have a chance to dance with her."

"Just do as what I say, okay? I will find a way for you to dance with her.

I promise. First, just take me as your partner."

I sighed and nodded. "All right. You're my partner for this week's ball."

I heard her clapping and screaming over the phone. "I can't wait for the ball!"

"You promised Lucinda," I warned her seriously. "That you'll solve this for me."

"I know, I know." She said inattentively. Then we hung up the phone promptly.

?

I had to admit that I couldn't stop wondering about Adela. Every moment I kept thinking like, 'Is she still upset?' or 'Should I talk to her first?' or 'Is she really dating Jeffrey?'

There were so many questions bubbling up in my head that I couldn't even count how many. I really wanted to ask her, but that moment when she yelled at me kept popping up whenever I try to open my mouth. I kept peeking at her face to see her expression, but she kept a straight face whenever I looked.

I had to ask someone about Adela, and the most appropriate person for this at that moment was Cathy, who is close to Adela, and who is never hesitant to say anything. After dinner, I called Cathy secretly.

"What's up?" She said, looking at me strangely. She seemed a little uncomfortable talking with me, but I didn't want to care about that then.

"Um," I thought in my head of how to start off conversation easily and finally opened my mouth. "Tomorrow is the ball, right?" I started.

She smiled and nodded excitedly. "Yes! And I am super excited! I can't believe they are even going to design my own dress! I can't wait until tomorrow," She jumped up and down for a several times, but stopped suddenly as if she thought of something. "Wait, but why did you call me out like this...oh, wait...are you going to ask me out to the ball?" She screamed with her eyes widened.

I quickly shook my head. "No Cathy...I just..."

"I am sorry. Charles," She waved her hand and said. "I already have a partner. I asked Lowell to go with me and he said okay. I just can't believe he accepted me as his partner!"

"Wait," I interrupted. "You are going with Lowell? What about Adela? Who is she going with?"

"It's none of your business, Charles." I heard a low voice behind me. It was Adela, still keeping her poker face.

"Come on Cathy. Let's go." Adela pulled Cathy's arm and tried to walk away from me.

"Adela," I called. She didn't look back, but I kept talking. "Are you inviting Jeffrey? Is that what is happening?"

Adela turned around sharply and glared at me. I never knew her beautiful green eyes could be so scary and pointy. Her eyes grew larger as her face turned scarlet with anger.

"Jeffrey Jeffrey... why are you so stuck with him? This is making me sick. Don't you dare talk about him ever again." She snapped and pulled Cathy's arm. But when they were about to leave, I continued talking.

"You should know that you won't see him at the ball," I shouted. "I'll put him on the blacklist and send it to the security."

"Shut up!" She turned around. I could see her tears gathered up in her eyes. "I hate you! I can't tell how miserable I am, going on quest with you."

I wanted to say something, but kept my mouth shut. I just couldn't believe I just asked her about Jeffrey.

I could feel my face burning up as I stood there watching her back.

I turned away from her and went upstairs. My hands were shaking as I nervously grabbed the doorknob and stepped into my room. I threw my whole body to the bed and inhaled loudly. I had no idea what to do, since my head was spinning and my heart was beating crazily.

I always have imagined Adela and me getting closer and all of a sudden it was all gone. And I was not sure I could get it all back on.

"If only I could rewind back to the time when we first met." I mumbled.

I heard a knock on my door. At a second, I hoped it was Adela, but I erased the thought when I heard a different voice.

"Your majesty, your suit has just arrived."

I unlocked the door and male maids came inside with a black suit, wrapped with a shiny plastic cover. They tore the wrap and lifted up for me to see the suit.

"It is a specially designed suit, your highness." They spinned it around for me to see the back side. I glanced at it passingly. I didn't want to face the suit. It felt like agony to me, looking at the nice suit and knowing the fact that I won't be dancing with Adela.

They hung the suit inside my closet as I nodded. They bowed and left the room.

I walked toward the closet and took out the suit.

"If only I could dance with Adela…" I mumbled as I put it back in.

Suddenly the phone rang across the room. I dragged myself towards the phone and received it.

"Hello?"

"Oh my god, Charlie," It was Lucinda with her voice more pitched than usual. "Did you send these for me?" she asked excitedly.

"Send what?"

"The dress," She squealed and giggled. "This is just gorgeous. Ooh, and there's more. A set of pearl earrings and a necklace! And…oh my god, stilettos!"

I could hear her jumping up and down with excitement.

"I think my mother sent them," I said blankly. "She said she is thankful of your father's donation of helping the poor last year."

"This is just so nice of her. Please say thank you to…oh, wait, no. Maybe I should tell her directly at the ball."

"Yeah, you should." I sighed.

"Are you all right?" she asked after a long term of silence.

"Do I sound like all right?" I murmured.

"Don't worry Charlie. You guys will be together again soon. This is not that huge. Trust me."

The Tension

Tomorrow came really fast. The colorful lights poured upon flowers and fountains of the garden, and the guards opened the gates to welcome the carriages. As the clock pointed 7, dozens of carriages started to enter endlessly. I watched the carriages through my room's window as they rolled through our gates.

I took out my suit from the closet and fiddled with it. I took a long hesitation before I finally wore the suit and stood in front of the mirror. It felt like I was wearing the tuxedo for the wedding without a bride. I looked okay, but all I could do was wondering about how Adela would be in the ball. She would look captivating surely enough. What would she wear? Who is she going to dance with? I couldn't stop wondering.

There was a knock on the door. "Your majesty, the ball is all ready."

I went downstairs to the ball. As I entered, I could see the sparkling chandeliers hanging on the ceiling and the long tables covered with red silk were rowed along the sides of the room with many kinds of dishes and in the middle was a dominant place for dancing. And in the front a large stage for instrument players and singers stood. The room was starting to be filled with lots of people as dozens kept entering. Some of them took notice of me and bowed or curtsied. I decided to wait Lucinda outside. As I came back out, I heard a voice from behind.

"Hey, Charles!" I turned around and saw Lucinda waving from a distance. She looked quite dazzling as her brownish black hair, curled up nicely, fell upon her back and across her chest. She was wearing a short dress which was mostly colored white but her sides black. The sparkles on her stilettos shone as she walked toward me.

I stared at her for a long time and finally opened my mouth.

"Wow," I said, flabbergasted. "You look just...gorgeous."

She twisted her long stretched legs and blushed coyly. "Thanks, you look great too."

I offered my arm for her to lock her arm with mine. We walked arm in arm and entered the ball.

As we just entered, everyone's eyes poured upon us. Some of them seemed to be whispering with each other and I could possibly guess that they were whispering, 'Why isn't prince with princess Monette?'

I could feel my face sweating, but I tried to look calm and satisfied. Simultaneously, I tried to look for Adela. I rolled my eyes around the room, but I couldn't find her. Maybe she is still not here, I thought.

"Hey, do you want to get some beverage? It's starting to get hot in here." She leaned over and whispered in my ear.

I nodded. There were lots of cups each filled with colorful beverage. Lucinda picked the red brandy from the table. I picked up another and we both took a sip.

The cold brandy smeared down my tongue and left a strong taste of liquor. I took another sip and continued to walk around the ball.

But I was still nervous thinking what I should do if I bump into Adela while we are locking our arms. My eyes kept searching for Adela, but still couldn't find her.

"Ahem," The voice rang through the microphone. Everyone's eyes turned to the stage and to the person who seemed like the host.

"Hello, ladies and gentlemen of the highest royals. This is your tonight's fun maker Jaden."

Everyone clapped. I decided to go to the backstage to look for Adela. She had to give a short speech with me before the start of the dance, but I was not sure if she was going to come upstage. As I expected, she was hiding behind the curtains in the backstage waiting for her time of speech. When our eyes met, she moved away her eyes and stared into spaces. I walked toward her and stood next to her.

I gained courage and smiled at her nervously. "Hi." I said, breaking the awkward silence.

She glanced at me coldly and rolled her eyes.

"Hi." She said hesitantly.

I secretly glanced at her. She looked wonderful in her velvet dress coming down to her knees. Her short curled hair looked ever so elegant. Her beauty was making my legs all wobbly.

"How's everything?" I asked again. I could feel my hands getting all sweaty, but I couldn't give up speaking to her.

She let out a small sigh. "All fine." She mumbled shortly.

"Do you have a partner?" I asked, feeling nervous if she was going to be mad at me again.

Suddenly the host called out Adela's name. She had to go upstage. Before she went upstage, she glared at me as if she had something to say, but she vanished into the light.

I peeked through the curtains and stared at her back. The host asked her how she felt and she said she feels marvelous tonight. The host continued asking about what she did during the quest and during training. She answered his questions calmly showing her straight face. And the last question made my heart stop.

"Wonderful, now may I ask you who your lucky guy is for tonight?"

I knew he asked that question expecting she would say my name, but there was a long silence as Adela kept her mouth shut. Her face started to go scarlet as she could hear whispers filling up the hall.

The host seemed a little flustered with Adela not saying anything.

He smiled and tried to cover it up. "Well, now ladies and gentlemen it's Prince Jones!" The claps rose up as I stepped up the stage and grabbed the microphone. As the applause stopped, the host asked pretty much the similar questions that he asked Adela a minute ago. And as well expected, he asked the same last question.

"So tell me, your highness. Who's your lucky gal?"

I hesitated. Should I call out Lucinda or should I just remain silent?

"I am, sir!" The voice from the audience pierced the silence. It was no wonder who shouted it. Everyone's eyes rolled upon Lucinda, who was standing in the middle, smiling and waving at me. At the same time, I regretted the moment that I accepted her to be my partner.

I could feel the glares from the audience and also lots of whispers which were quite certainly about us. I could almost hear them saying, "Oh my god, Charles and Adela aren't partners? What happened? Did Charles dump her?"

The host seemed as he was thinking of what to say to stop the awkwardness. He took a long moment of thinking and continued on talking.

"Oh well, there's your lucky gal your highness. According to my notice that lovely lady is…Ms. Goldsmith, is that right your highness?"

"Um, yes…" I answered blankly as I took a short glance of Adela's face. Her face was still red, but she seemed as she was trying to keep her face straight, so it was still hard for me to read her mind.

The short interviews ended swiftly and Adela and I could get off the stage as quick as I wished. Lucinda was waiting for me just below the stage stairs. She looked at Adela first and snatched my hand.

"Come on, let's go! The music is going to start in any minute and we should go dance!"

I couldn't resist her force and I had to be pulled into the dance with her. Everything was going on as crazily fast as I had no time to think about anything. As we stood in the middle of the dance floor, many people's eyes were, once again, shooting on us. I wanted to turn my head to look for Adela, but I couldn't turn my head while I was dancing. With one hand on Lucinda's shoulder and the other on her waist, we danced slowly by the rhythm of the classic that was played with the violin and cello. Their music sounded melancholy and I didn't know why but it reminded me more of Adela.

The collaboration of cello and violin was so beautiful, but as for me, I desperately hoped that it would end quickly so I could go find Adela. The more we spinned while dancing, the more my brain got addled. Fortunately, the music ended fast. Everyone in the floor clapped and changed partners. I whispered to Lucinda that we should take a rest for this turn.

As we got out of the dance floor, I looked around to find Adela, but it was just too hard finding her in this enormous room filled with hundreds of people.

"Wait here, I'll go look for Adela okay?" I said to Lucinda.

Lucinda smiled and made a gesture at me which seemingly meant 'go ahead'. I looked around and searched and searched, but she was nowhere to be found.

"Where is she?" I growled frustratingly as suddenly, my eyes met someone I was familiar with. My eyes caught Lowell talking with someone while looking around the ball, but he moved away as he spotted me as well. I ran across the floor, weaving my way through hundreds of people. I could see Lowell grabbing a woman's arm and moving from where they were standing. Maybe that woman is Adela, I thought as I fixed my eyes on them and kept following.

At last, I caught them as they stood trapped between the wall and me.

I first grabbed the woman who was dragged along and turned her around. It was Cathy.

"Cathy," I looked at her, stunned. "It was you."

Lowell tried to pull her away, but before that, with my other hand I grabbed Lowell strongly. "Hey," I yelled. Our eyes met again. He always offends me, but I squished my anger and calmly asked Cathy. "Where's Adela?"

Cathy stared at me for a minute and finally opened her mouth.

"Where's your partner?"

"Partner who?"

"You know that girl…what was her name…Ms. Goldsmith…wasn't it?"

What Cathy said made me more regretful about taking Lucinda as my partner.

I sighed and begged. "Where is Adela? I need to know."

She seemed to hesitate a little. "Adela went up to her room right after her speech," She said. "She told us she wants to be alone tonight. We tried to convince her that she is the reason why we are holding the ball, but she wouldn't listen. So Lowell took her upstairs and came down just a few minutes ago."

After I heard what Cathy said, I let go of her arm and ran. I could hear Cathy screaming at me, "Don't offend her too much though!"

I ran out the ball and sprinted up the stairs. I could feel my heart thumping wildly inside my chest as I ran like I lost my mind. When I arrived at the second floor, I could see the door far away. I ran and ran until I finally reached the door. My lungs were sore and burning and my neck was dry from harsh running. The cold touch of the door knob ran through my bones and laid goosebumps on my back. I slowly turned it around. The door slid open.

I peeked inside. It was dark, but I could see a string of dim light shining from the balcony, along with a silhouette of a beautiful lady, Adela.

She was sitting on a chair with something on a tea table next to her. As I stepped closer, I could see that on the table were a bottle of wine and a several wine glasses. I could feel the breeze, coming through the chink of the balcony door. As I slowly walked toward the balcony door and slightly opened it, the door made a squeaky sound, but she didn't look around to check who it was. I slowly walked around her and sat on the opposite side of her. Still, she wouldn't look at me.

I quietly grabbed a glass and poured a little from the bottle and at the same time, she turned her head and looked at me.

"What are you doing here?" She asked, stunned.

"Well, I just wanted to see you."

"Go away. I don't need you." She said coldly.

"Why are you being so grumpy huh?"

She didn't say anything, staring into spaces without looking at me, so I continued on talking.

"It's because you believe that I stole the letters and I didn't ask you out to the ball. Is that right?"

There was another silence filling the breeze.

I sighed. "Adela…I believe everything starts from rough, and I believe we can relate that to our situation here,"

She turned her head and looked at me. Her dazzling green eyes shone brightly in the moonlight. I could see her eyes were little teary.

I swallowed and continued. "Look. I am telling you this because I still believe we can get back together like before. Adela, I am terribly sorry about the letters. I mean it really, but you can't just be dragged by that stalker forever. Because you deserve someone way better than him: someone who cares about you and loves you more than anything, someone who loves you in a proper way, not just requiring you for love."

Adela looked at me seeming puzzled. "Well, who would that be?" She asked.

I suddenly let out a chuckle. "Adela," I said smiling. "You know what? No offense but sometimes you are really, really dense."

"What are you talking about? I am…not dense."

"Oh, yes you are. You are just so dense you don't even know what's happening."

Adela raised her voice. "I do know what's happening, you freak."

"No you don't."

"I do! I know as least something."

"No, you are just…"

Suddenly, my tie was gripped and pulled by a huge force, as well as my whole body. And I froze as something crashed onto my lips.

It was Adela, standing up as she held my tie and locked her lips into mine. And soon I realized; she was kissing me.

All I knew was her lips felt soft and tender. Her warm breath, tasting grape-sweet, tickled my nostrils. I kissed her back as I leaned to her and folded my hand with hers. That moment, nothing could be sweeter than this.

A moment later, she let go of the grasp on my tie and stopped the ecstasy. I slowly opened my eyes and looked at Adela, but she didn't look back. She sat down like nothing happened and seemed as if she felt embarrassed. I couldn't hold back my smile from coming up on my face.

I hesitated a moment and finally opened my mouth.

"Will you dance with me?" I said and took out my hand.

She bit her lips and shyly laid her hand onto mine. She smiled beautifully and we both left the balcony.

Two is Better than One

I had to introduce Lucinda to Adela and tell Adela several times to make her believe that Lucinda and I are just friends. She kept suspecting on us, but she finally seemed to be persuaded as Lucinda kindly explained what happened. When Adela heard what we had planned, she pinched me playfully and smiled as a meaning of forgiving.

Suddenly, I thought of an incredible idea and whispered to Adela. At first she shook her head shyly, but I kept convincing her with my idea. She gave in eventually and we both ran up the stage and stopped the music.

Everyone down the stage stopped the dance and looked at us. We received the microphones. People clapped as I cleared my throat.

I nervously took a deep breath and started talking. "Hello again, I am terribly sorry about interrupting the fun. Adela and I have something to say,"

I took another deep breath and continued. "Adela and I were going through a hard time even until the beginning of this ball. It was my entire fault actually. Thankfully, she came back to me and we are back together."

People clapped and cheered. Adela giggled and smiled at me.

"Thank you very much," I said. "Also we are here to bless this moment with you and, as a matter of fact, we decided to sing a duet on this stage. Sadly, we didn't have time to practice, but we hope you enjoy. The title of the song is 'Two is better than one'."

They applauded once more and the applause quietened down as the ensemble started playing the music. I began singing the first part and glanced at Adela. She was looking down as she felt nervous and embarrassed. I was also afraid thinking what if she doesn't sing along with me, but to my surprise when the music reached her part, she lifted her head and let out her amazing voice. Her voice rang through the room and captivated every one of them in the ball including me. Everyone seemed to be amazed like me. As we sang together I reached out and grabbed her hand. We stood right in the middle of the stage and looked down at the people.

Suddenly, there was someone who ran inside the ball. It was Lowell and Cathy breathing heavily from running. They both stared at us vacantly. I noticed Lowell staring at me and I didn't know why, but his stare seemed cold and it was pretty much close to glaring.

As Adela and I finished the duet perfectly, the audience gave a long ovation. I could see Cathy smiling from far away and clapping with the audience.

But Lowell didn't clap. He kept glaring at us or probably at me. But I could feel this little excitement similar to victory deep in my mind as I noticed his disappointment, but I still couldn't find the reason why he was disappointed with me.

After we vowed and curtsied, we climbed down the stage. Adela ran into Cathy and they hugged each other delightfully.

"You guys were awesome!" Cathy squealed and jumped up and down. "You guys look so great together! Lowell and I are so happy for you. Right? Lowell?"

We all looked at Lowell's face which was still distorted. He made an awkward smile and nodded. Adela smiled and hugged Lowell as well, but he stood there frozen and didn't hug her back.

Adela pulled my arm and gestured to go dancing. I chuckled and got pulled in the middle of the dance floor. As we waited for the music to start, suddenly a group of band came upstage and played rock type music. Everyone started dancing crazily and so did we, jumping up and down. And from far away, I could see Lowell, still staring at us blankly. But I was too focused on dancing to notice a drop of tear falling from his face.

Leaving

I opened my eyes. In front of my eyes I could see the ceiling of my bedroom. The sunlight was peeking through the gap between the curtains of the window and brightening it up.

I was in my room, lying down on my bed as usual. I closed my eyes and rewound the time back to yesterday. The picture of Adela and me dancing, singing the song and the moment we first kissed kept appearing in front of my eyes.

As I pictured Adela, my heart started beating crazily and my face felt like burning up. I squeezed the pillow beside me and tried to calm it down, but it wouldn't slow down.

I decided to get out of bed and take a morning shower. I looked up the clock. It was 5:30 a.m. and I had plenty of time to prepare. I grabbed the towel and went to the bathroom.

After about 10 minutes I finished the shower and threw my undried body on the bed. The water soaked into my bed but I didn't really care.

I couldn't stop thinking about that enchanting moment. It was dominating my whole brain. It was my first kiss anyway so I found it irresistible. I shook my head to get out of the intensity of excitement, but it was no use.

I got out of my room and walked to Adela's room. As I knocked on her door, she opened it.

She came out of her room and grinned shyly. "Hey." She whispered.

I held her hand gently. "Good morning." I said.

She seemed a little surprised at me suddenly holding her hand, but she giggled and squeezed it. "We are finally leaving Elsmiere today."

"Yeah I know. I can't believe you finally mastered everything I taught you for the past few…"

"We," She interrupted. "It's 'we'."

The savory scent of hot bread danced around my nostrils. As we sat down, the servants prepared us rice soup and a loaf of honey bread. I asked where my parents were, and he replied that they already finished their breakfast earlier because they were busy. We thought about waiting for Lowell and Cathy, but we decided to eat first and look for them later.

Cathy came down to the dining room right after the time we finished our meal. She was still in her pajamas, looking like she was not fully awake.

"You guys already finished breakfast?" She said, yawning. "Gosh, then I have to eat alone."

"Where's Lowell?" Adela asked.

"I don't know," Cathy grabbed her spoon and squished some of her soup into her mouth. "I knocked on his door, but he didn't reply. Maybe he is still sleeping."

"We'll bring him here Cathy. Wait here okay?"

Adela and I went up to Lowell's room. I didn't want to go wake him up, but since Adela was going I went with her.

She knocked on the door. There was no answer.

"Lowell!" She raised her voice and knocked harder. "Are you still sleeping? Lowell?"

She knocked and knocked, but there was no answer.

Adela bit her lip and looked at me. "Maybe he's in the bathroom and cannot hear me knocking." She said nervously.

We waited. Gosh, I just can't think well of him in any way. Why does he have to keep us waiting like this? What is he doing in there?

Plenty of time passed and we were going to be late if he doesn't come out this moment. Adela knocked on his door again and called out his name.

There was no sound coming behind the door. We decided to ask one of the guards to open the door. So the guard brought a key and opened it.

As the door opened, I could feel the cool breeze swishing from the widely opened balcony. The bed was all messed up with pillows and blankets all over it. We could find his goods, but there was no one.

Adela's face turned pale as a sheet of paper. She spotted something on the desk and lifted up with her trembling hands.

I nervously walked toward her.

Her hands trembled even harder as I stepped closer. She looked up to me with her teary eyes that were about to burst into tears.

"Look."

-continued on book 2